# THE CREATURE WITHIN

# THE CREATURE WITHIN

RACHAEL
MACPHERSON-WOOD

# Contents

# Prologue

The city was dull and the buildings looked like skeletons in the evening sky. Beams of light from the setting sun shot through holes in the skyline and illuminated the streets. The streets I grew up on, torn apart and left to rot. Nature had started to reclaim its place, even though most things had shrivelled up and died before being given the chance to thrive. It was easy to tell there was still radiation lingering.

I needed to get home soon. After the war, it was not safe to be outside after dark. The sun was setting, and I still had a thirty-minute walk home. Weighted down by the new supplies I had just stolen from our local supermarket, what was left of it, anyway.

There was a noise behind me and the hair on my neck stood on its end. My hand gripped tightly around my makeshift spear. The metal bar was cold against my skin. My heart throbbed in my chest. I felt eyes watching me, but when I turned, I saw nothing. My eyes darted around, but all

I could see were the ruined buildings, trying to stand their ground, too stubborn to fall. The stench of decay was everywhere. I let out a breath I didn't realise I was holding and loosened my grip on the weapon.

*Must have been an animal.* I tried to reassure myself. I continued my walk home, slightly more hurried as the atmosphere darkened. The sky turned grey, and rain clouds formed in the distance. A shiver ran up my spine.

Heavy footsteps sounded behind me and this time when I turned, my body was frozen with fear.

# Chapter 1

*Melody*

I felt the sting of every rain drop as it collided with my body. Like an ice-cold mist covering me. My body felt stiff, bones and muscles aching the way I had become so accustomed to.

It was like this every time.

Every time I woke up after I had shifted, with only spots of memory from the night before.

I needed to get home. Home. That felt like such a strange concept.

After the war there wasn't much of a home to go to. Especially when I started shifting. Which was becoming increasingly difficult to hide from my family. I didn't want them to know, to worry or to be in danger. Who knows what would happen to them, or to me, if anyone found out. This was the third time I had shifted in two weeks. It was getting worse, more frequent. Each time I woke up after being shifted, I felt less human.

The light almost blinded me as I tried to open my eyes. Squinting, I rolled to my side and took in my surroundings. How did I always manage to find myself on the outskirts of the city? Like the animal inside me was trying to escape, running for the forest.

I moved all my weight onto my arms and pushed myself up to sit on my knees. My body let out a groan as I stretched my back and cracked my neck to either side. I rolled my neck around and lifted my arms above my head. I looked around, hoping to find some remnants of the night before. As always, nothing. My clothes were gone, and my arms and hands were covered in blood. I searched my body for any wounds or scrapes.

*It's not my blood.* I thought to myself. Relieved at first, then I shuddered as the realisation hit that it was someone else's.

I missed the days where my biggest worries were my homework, getting to sleep in on weekends, or worrying about what I was going to do with my future. Instead of trying to survive every damn day.

Shivering and stiff, I began the slow walk home. I warily took each step, still adjusting to my human form again. Sending aches along my legs and up the muscles of my back. I found one of the five duffle bags I'd hidden around the city. It was filled with spare clothes, small weapons, water and some simple medication and bandages. Things that would tie me over until I could make it home. When the shifts started happening, I would wake up lost, naked and in need of water. I was always a little banged up at first too, no knowledge of the night before or how I obtained the injuries.

Sometimes, like today, I was covered in blood that was not my own. So, I had packed a few things and hidden them in places I knew would be safe.

After a new set of clothes and a whole bottle of water, I was on my way home. My mother and brother would be at home, the former none the wiser I was ever gone.

My mother, before all of this, was a florist. My father bought her a little shop in the city. It gave her something to do while my father worked long hours as a doctor. She didn't need the money from working and I often caught her giving the flowers away for free.

She did it because she loved the feeling it gave her, to make someone else smile. She truly was a people-person. She was the epitome of beauty and grace. Dancing and singing around her shop, long dresses flowing and smiling ear to ear. She was a vision. Beautiful long black hair, trailing below her waist. Dark as night and curling at the ends naturally.

She had the loveliest eyes. They were a deep blue, like the ocean and her skin was porcelain white.

She wore a perfect smile and treated every living thing with care and wonder.

I remember spending a few hours after school at her shop, helping her put together bouquets and arrangements. Watching her dance around the room, singing or humming. She took up so much space, in the best way possible.

But not anymore.

Now, if she builds up the courage to leave her room, she barely speaks a word to me or my younger brother.

She lost herself after my father died.

After he was killed.

He was a doctor and volunteered to work on the front-line when the war broke out. He was deployed there for almost a year before he died. We only saw him every few weeks.

There was a mysterious explosion in their medical ward, killing many and injuring so many more. Then people started to *change*, and he was killed by one of his patients.

When he didn't come home, she became a shell of a human. Stopped eating, lay in bed for days on end and lost all hope. I resented her for it. For failing to hold the family together when we needed her the most.

She lost her husband, but we lost our father and she just stopped caring.

I was 18 when it happened and my brother, Daniel, was only 16.

Daniel has always been smart. Smarter than me. He had such a bright future ahead of him.

At the age of 14, before everything happened, he was making small inventions in his room. Always tinkering away. Making silly little things at first. Tools and equipment to help my father at work. Little knick-knacks for our father to take to work with him.

One invention was a coffee warmer, so his coffee wouldn't go cold while he saw patients. He was always busying himself with inventions. His mind just knew how to put things together to make interesting contraptions.

Then, at 15, during the war, he made a cauteriser that was able to fuse together large wounds with minimal damage. The army took the idea and spent thousands of dollars to make duplicates. Daniel was praised for his work but never compensated.

Daniel had just turned 16 when my father was killed and when my mother stopped caring for us. It didn't take us long to realise we were going to have to grow up fast. He would stay up late most nights, creating some piece of equipment that would help us around the house.

I started leaving the house on my own and searching the streets for things that would help with Daniel's work. I would often trade our household items for food or other things we needed.

Then, Daniel started making and selling weapons to the army and anyone else who could afford it.

As I rounded the corner near my house, I could see the roller metal shutters still covering the windows. Daniel had covered the house in minor home security. Not cameras or anything like that, but protection on the windows and reinforcing the doors and locks.

Most neighbouring homes had been looted and ruined in the weeks following the explosion. All our windows were covered with automatic shutters, set up on a timer; they closed at six o'clock at night and didn't open again until six the next morning.

The house wasn't anything special. Single story, with a basement, red brick, three-bedroom house. The contents were even less notable. Especially since I had sold or traded most of our things during the first few weeks following the explosion. All our childhood memories from growing up in this house had been tarnished in the blink of an eye. We kept all our family photos but I packed them away in boxes and hid them in the ceiling. In case the house was attacked and looted. That happened a lot in those first few weeks. Buildings being torn apart for the contents, no matter how meaningless.

Those few weeks were so quiet. We went about our days trying to get through. Trying to survive.

We had no idea that the worst was yet to come.

We heard rumours that people who fought on the front line were *changing*. My mother sent word to my father, begging him to come home. But he was killed before he got the letter.

After the explosion, people became different. It was the radiation that mutated them. The explosion sent a shockwave across the city, affecting more and more people.

Their bodies mutated and shifted form. Some were affected more than others.

Before we knew about the mutations, there were army troops who came crashing through our neighbourhood, *looking for sick people*, they said.

They door knocked every house to find those who were showing signs of change. People were being ripped from their homes, kicking and screaming. Dragged into the trucks parked on the road and locked in until the searches were completed. Families were torn apart.

And in the beginning, no one knew why but as time went on, more people became affected by the radiation, and it was hard to hide it anymore.

*Precautions.* They told the rest of us. *To keep you safe from any danger.*

I waited out the back of our house. Choosing to sit under the veranda on the worn wooden chair, I picked at the dirt and blood under my nails and closed my eyes as I tried to remember the last thing that happened before I shifted.

I was here, at home, in the kitchen. Daniel and I were arguing about his weapons, again. I hated it when he sold them. People were killing, just for the sake of it. Using this whole disaster as an excuse to purge. Who knew people could be so cruel.

After the argument I left to clear my head, I went into the city. That was all I could strain my brain to remember. I threw my hands in the air in defeat. It was useless, I never remembered much from my time when I was shifted.

I reached above my head and stretched and the shutters began opening. I turned around to see Daniel looking out at me from the kitchen window. Glass of water in his hands and that same expressionless face he always wore.

*Great, now I need to explain myself.* I thought as I got up from the chair and opened the back door to let myself in.

I looked at the clock on the wall and did a quick calculation that I had been gone one day. I left the house yesterday, early afternoon and did not come home until now.

"Where have you been?" Daniel stood with his arms crossed over his chest, sipping from his water, "You look terrible and you know it's not safe after dark." His face showed no emotion.

He leaned on the kitchen counter with one leg crossed over the other, looking completely unbothered.

"I know" I said, "I'm fine." I pushed past him and headed for the bathroom.

I needed to shower, to wash away the smell of last night. He grumbled something under his breath as I passed him. I was grateful that he knew not to pry.

I walked down the dim hallway, past Daniel's room, my room and stopped in front of my mother's closed door. Part of me wanted to open it, walk in and see if she was up and dressed. See if there was any part of her that remained. But I knew I would only break my own heart, let myself down.

She was not in there anymore, just her vessel. So, I continued to the bathroom.

I stared into the mirror and hardly recognised myself anymore. I removed my clothes and examined my body to see if I had any injuries, but there was nothing. My long, golden hair almost looked brown with how dirty it was.

Daniel was right, I did look terrible.

Dark circles framed my blue eyes, evidence of my exhaustion. My eyes were the same ocean blue as my mothers, the only part of me that looked anything like her. My golden-brown hair looked just like my fathers; straight, thick and when taken care of, shone like the sun. My figure had become noticeably leaner since we were living off scraps and I was walking and running so often.

I stayed in the shower for longer than I should. Another thing for Daniel to bicker with me about. He had somehow rigged the pipe systems, so we had enough warm water running for three showers a day. One each. Although, I know my mother hadn't used hers in some time.

When I strode back to the lounge area, clean clothes and hair braided tightly to the back, I could see the basement light on.

Daniel must have been working down there. He had transformed the basement into his workspace. I often found the light on at night, when I couldn't sleep. I suppose he couldn't either. The walls were covered in metal objects, some things I recognised, others I didn't. He had three work benches; all used for different things. Each of the tables were covered in bits of metal, plastic, objects half made and some papers with Daniel's handwriting scribbled on them. I didn't have a clue what he was making, but I knew I wasn't allowed to touch anything. It looked like piles of mess to me, but he said everything had its place and he knows exactly where that is. I took him a cup of coffee, a peace offering for disappearing all night, again. I placed it on the workbench he wasn't using and went to sit in the old chair near the stairs. The room was lit with dusty yellow lighting and Daniel wore a head torch that lit up the objects he held in front of his face.

"What are you working on?" I asked, sipping my own coffee. Definitely not a barista made caramel latte, but it got the job done.

He didn't look up from his work, his face intense on whatever it was that he was doing. Steady hands, fusing two objects together. "Where were you last night?" He replied without looking in my direction.

I understood what he meant, both questions offered a *need-to-know* answer.

I nodded, a clear indication that this conversation was not going to happen. I stood from the chair and started for the stairs.

As I made it to the top of the stairs, I heard Daniel say, almost under his breath "Just be careful Mel."

I felt shame wash over me. I didn't have the courage to talk to him about this right now. I said nothing as I turned and closed the basement door behind me.

Of course I wanted to tell him, I knew he would figure it out soon enough. I wasn't sure how much longer I wanted to keep it from him either. We have had neighbours disappear into the night, families wondering what happened to them. But over time, we found out they either got captured by the Snatchers and taken to the underground lab for who knows what, or they became something entirely inhuman.

Either way, no one ever saw them again.

I went straight to my room and closed the door. My room was small, a single bed pushed into the corner, the same floral sheets as I always had. A bookshelf in the opposite corner filled with books. Most of them I had read, but some of them I'd bought for the pretty front cover and never picked up again. I had a study desk in between the bed and bookshelf and a small mirror leaned up against the wall. It wasn't much, but I felt safe here.

I paced my room, my head started spinning. I wondered if I should go back down there and tell Daniel everything. When my thoughts were running in circles, I fell to my bed. The sun was still shining through my curtains and despite it being morning, I curled into a ball and pulled my covers high over me. Sleep took me swiftly as I sank into the mattress.

~~~

*Everything was dark, I was looking through what felt like binoculars. Night vision? I was searching for something, and I could smell it in the air. My heart felt strong and I could feel it pumping blood through my veins. My senses were overloaded. I could feel the ground humming beneath me, smell things I hadn't before, and the wind spoke in song to me. Whispering.*

*I started running, I knew where I was going and I was moving fast. My stomach turned over as I lifted my snout to smell the sweet iron in the air. My body was stronger than I had ever felt it, my bones felt solid and my head was clear. I rounded the corner and saw the maimed animal laying there. I lunged forward and it screamed under me as I ripped its skin from its body, exposing more than just muscle and bone. My eyes darted around as I shoved large lumps of muscle into my mouth. I could hear voices nearing, so I slipped into the shadows and waited.*
~~~

I jolted awake and sat up straight. My forehead glistening, my sheets drenched with sweat. Still panicked, I looked around the room, familiarising myself with where I was.

*Dream, it was just a dream.* I thought to myself. *I am in my bedroom and I am safe.*

I held my chest and counted to ten slowly. Deep breaths in and slow breaths out. I had been having these nightmares for some time now. Since the shifting began. I called them nightmares, because the thought of them being memories made me sick to my stomach.

The shutters were down and only a slight hint of moonlight shone through the edge of where they connected with the window. I slept all day. I figured there were still a few hours until sunrise but I decided to wander from my room and find something to eat. I had slept through dinner, and my stomach grumbled to remind me.

Coming into the kitchen it was almost pitch black, but I knew my way around this house with my eyes closed, so it was no issue avoiding things that may have been in my path. I found the fruit bowl and picked an apple blindly.

One of my favourite memories was years ago. My mother and I had planted a few trees in the backyard, one of which was an apple tree. We tried to make some vegetable patches too, but they didn't survive the first winter. The apple tree was the only one still producing fruit. I was thankful for it, as it had saved us from going without food many times in the last year. Not that my mother has eaten an apple, or barely anything since losing my father.

I sat down on the couch, careful not to bump the round table to the left and listened. I listened to the quiet on the other side of the house walls. Something almost enticing about how quiet it was. Daring me to step outside. Wild animals didn't stick around much, I assumed they'd been eaten or scared and run off. Some very brave, or stupid ones did linger though.

A scream sounded, close enough to startle me. Instinctively, I got into a crouched position. I wasn't sure why I hid down, no one could see me in here, but I felt safer closer to the ground. I listened hard, closing my eyes. Had I imagined it?

The high-pitched scream came again, and I jolted. This time it was louder as though the person, the woman, was running this direction, down our street.

I could just make out her panicked pleas for help, and I went to the window to see if I could see anything between the shutters. Daniel had done such a good job that I could only see small stars of light coming through.

Daniel appeared at my back, giving me a subtle hush as he came to the window too. We stood there silently for a moment while the commotion outside continued. She was further away now, and no longer alone. Vehicles had arrived and the Snatchers' footsteps were quick as they tried to apprehend her. We could hear the violence that came with them. Every time their weapons connected with her. Her screams of pain and pleas for help dwindled. I winced at the thought of it. How scared she must be. They had hunted her down and finally caught up to her, capturing her and taking her to the lab, I assumed. Some of the weapons made zapping noises and some had a sole purpose to be used with brute force. Weapons I was almost sure Daniel had created and sold to the Snatchers.

"We should help her." I said under my breath to Daniel. Who was now sitting on the floor next to me, with his back against the wall.

"No." He replied a little short. And I knew he was right, there was nothing we could do to help.

When someone shifted, they shifted back and forth between human form and creature form until they didn't shift back anymore, they stayed in their mutated form permanently. They became something so unhuman that it couldn't shift back. Left to roam the streets of the city, killing as it pleased. Or they were hunted down by the Snatchers and taken to the underground lab for testing. I wasn't sure which was worse.

The Snatchers, even though they technically worked for the army, were a very uncontrolled group of people. People who made it their life's work to destroy all creatures. They captured the creatures and took them under the city. Those who didn't get brought to the lab, were left to the mercy of the Snatchers. The army was put together just before the war. The original army was told to step down and a man, who people called the General, took over. He had his own men, his own base and his very own way of doing things. They fought over territory for just over six months, before the General had the opposition begging for mercy. He had very unorthodox ways of prevailing. They were an extremely secretive group of people. Feared by many.

Everyone was shocked by the explosion that happened in their very own quarters. Once the mutations began, they purpose built a huge laboratory for the creatures. Those creatures who stayed in their form were harder to catch, harder to kill. They lost all sense of who they were before shifting, becoming rabid monsters.

People were offered rewards for tipping off anyone who shifted. Given money, or food, or special privileges. Tough times had people turning on one another.

As the trucks drove off, the night became silent again, except for the few growls and grumbles far off in the distance. Daniel and I returned to our bedrooms, not speaking a word to one another.

# Chapter 2

The shutters cranked open, startling me awake. I hadn't realised I'd dozed off again, after what happened last night. It wasn't the first time we heard something like that happen, but it was just as unnerving each time. I was grateful for the dreamless sleep between then and now. The sun was peeping through the low trees, and the morning air was fresh. I got dressed quickly and headed outside to investigate the events from last night. Daniel must have had the same idea as me, because he was already heading for the front door when I came down the hallway.

"Who do you think it was?" I said, as I caught up with him.

"I know as much information as you, Melody." Sarcasm was his favourite language. Even though Daniel was younger than me by about 18 months, he stood a whole foot taller than me. Broad shoulders and a strong build. He shared my golden hair and had striking hazel eyes. He reminded me so much of our father.

I stayed silent as we walked down the street. There was a trail of dripping blood heading one way down the street, past our house and down the road. We followed it and came to a stop in front of a rich crimson puddle. Too much for any normal person to survive. It was obvious that the woman put up a fight, the blood was spilled everywhere. And there were all sorts of animal prints, weaving patterns in and out of the dark red pool. They were curious about the commotion too, I suppose.

"I didn't think there were still so many animals around." Said Daniel, crouched down on the edge of the blood.

"I don't think they're just animals Dan. Look." I pointed to the large imprint on the ground. Five spindly fingers and the ball of the print being much larger than mine or Daniel's.

"That's probably her print. She must have shifted." He said bluntly.

"I wonder what they do with them once they've captured them." A lump formed in my throat. *Captured me.* I thought, my eyes stung as I tried to block it out.

"I don't think you want to know Mel. Horrible things." Daniel stood up. His hazel eyes looked gold as the morning sun reflected off them. His dusty blonde hair looked like a mop on top of his head; I must remember to cut that for him.

He walked slowly back towards our house, turning to say, "I'm going to be out today, for most of the day. So don't expect me home 'till later." He brushed his hand through his hair and turned back towards the house, not waiting for my response.

"Okay, no worries." I replied anyway. We barely spoke about what the other did during the day anymore. I knew Daniel travelled into the city most days, but I didn't have a clue what he was doing. I wasn't sure I wanted to know. It was clear we were both hiding things, keeping secrets from the other. Only, my secret would land me in that lab, where horrible things happen. I shuddered at the thought.

The days were growing repetitive. I would wake up, inspect any events from the night prior, have a drab breakfast of any kind of tinned thing I found in our cupboard and then head out at some stage to explore. Seeing if I could find anything, something new to spark my interest. I only stopped back at home to check on my mother and try to get her to eat or shower. Sometimes that wasn't until dinner and some days I stayed home to tend to our pathetic garden or read my books inside. Those days were always my favourite. They felt somewhat normal and my mind didn't race as much.

To my surprise, when I got home just before lunch, my mother was standing in the lounge room, looking into the backyard.

Her clothes hung off her body, she had lost so much weight. Her long dark hair trailed well past her shoulders, just above her hips, falling flat and without shape. Her skin was so pale, dark circles encased her deep blue eyes. They were sunken and without life. Cheekbones, collarbones and I could only assume her ribs too, all on show from the months of grief. She looked nothing like the mother I remembered. My mother would be shocked at the sight of the woman standing in front of me now.

"Mum?" I approached her more cautiously than if I was out exploring the city.

She turned in one smooth motion as if I had startled her out of a daydream. But she said nothing. She stood with one hand clasped tightly around her necklace. My father had given it to her when she gave birth to me. It was a beautiful gold heart with a picture of them from their wedding day inside. She never took it off, not a single day since she received it.

"Are you okay? Can I get you some water, or something to eat?" I held the palms of my hands out towards her, as if I was going to catch her frail body if she moved. Without speaking, she placed her hand in mine and nodded, allowing me to take her into my arms and guide her to the armchair.

I made her a sad excuse for lunch, some tinned beans and an apple from our tree. I didn't take my eyes off her, scared she might disappear in front of my eyes. But she sat in her chair and waited patiently. She ate the food with no complaints and I watched her from the couch opposite. Once she had finished, I took her bowl, and she stalked down the hallway to her room again.

I sighed with disappointment. My body fluttered with hope every time I saw her out of the bedroom, but every time she reminded me why I had no faith in her to begin with. She wasn't my mother anymore, just a shell of a human that I sometimes took care of. It was infuriating. We went through the same thing. Daniel and I lost our father and yet we are out here trying to survive, while she let herself waste away. We were trying to get on with whatever life is out there for us. A new life. She didn't care whether she lived or died. We lost both our parents in that war, and I resented her for it.

After grumbling to myself while cleaning the dishes, I headed back out into the city. I needed to get out of the house and there was a building I wanted to check out that I had seen a few days ago.

I retrieved my makeshift spear, one that I had made, not Daniel. I remember him laughing at me and refusing to give me any pointers while I struggled welding a large blade onto the metal bar. I packed myself some food and two bottles of water. Fixed my hair into a tight braid towards the back of my head and set off.

The city was gloomy, there was no life, except for the scurrying few animals that stayed behind, sticking to the shadows and scurrying away with my presence. I wondered where they went at night to stay safe. The streets were littered with old rubbish, ruins from the collapsing buildings and I'm sure there were more rotting carcasses than my eyes allowed me to see. The city smelt like it was decaying. People who died in the beginning were left where they fell as others panicked to save themselves. It was within those first few weeks where the bodies piled up the most. Then they slowly started to disappear, the ones that were too far into decomposition were left to continue their natural cycle. Leaving the streets covered in rotting bodily fluids and a stench that made breathing too hard. Over time though, it went away or it just got more tolerable.

I was always on alert when exploring the city, but it had been so long since I had encountered a creature that I almost forgot they were out here. Though there were the occasional reminders, pools of blood or footprints no human or animal could create.

As I rounded the corner, the building I was searching for came into view. It looked like it was once a medical centre. The walls were once white and rendered but now stained and cracked with neglect. And the sign for the front had fallen and was now covering most of the original entrance. The glass windows had been smashed and damaged, no doubt due to the looting at the beginning of everything. I walked around the front twice, looking for my best entry point. It looked like I'd have to climb through one of the broken windows and it would be a tight fit. I removed my backpack and lay it on top of the broken glass window as a barrier between me and the shards of glass.

As I suspected, it was a tight fit, I had to let my breath out as I squeezed in and popped out the other side. I grabbed my backpack, retrieving the small flashlight I had in one of the many pockets and I started to look around. Every step was considered and I was careful not to make a noise. I didn't know what was in here, if anything, but I didn't want to make myself known either way.

The front room was some sort of reception. I could make out the overturned desk and the seats that I imagined used to be lined up in neat rows.

It reminded me of my fathers' old workplace, before he volunteered to help on the frontline, he had his own practice. I would sometimes go to his office after school and sit in the staff room. Waiting for him to finish work. His receptionist would always bring me a sweet treat and make sure I was comfortable while I waited. My father always wanted me to follow in his footsteps and become a doctor, like him.

I followed the corridor to the back rooms, where it looked like three separate consult rooms and then a staff lunchroom. It had a small table, chairs, a fridge and a small kitchenette. This room was almost untouched. As if it was paused in time. The fridge was open and had been emptied, but the rest of the room was left to age gracefully. With a layer of dust covering most surfaces, my body eased at the thought of no one being in here for some time. The calendar was still hanging on the wall. It had been almost 15 months since the explosion happened. Since people lost all sense of right and wrong. For almost 15 months Daniel and I had been barely surviving.

I moved back into the corridor and headed towards the closed door at the end. The sunlight from outside was peeking through the windows and doorways. It wasn't as dark as it could've been, although I was still happy to have my flashlight. It was dusty and quiet as I made my way down the hall, spotlight fixed on the door. I reached out for the doorhandle and grasped the cold metal sphere, slowly turning my wrist.

*Locked.* I thought as I tried to twist the handle again. I turned back down the corridor, my flashlight illuminating the way. I didn't think it was worth making a lot of noise for whatever was behind that door. I crept back towards the window I used to break in. Defeated. I had gotten very used to keeping quiet and knowing when to give up.

*Well, this was a royal waste of my time,* I thought, I wasn't sure what I was expecting to find here, but finding nothing was very underwhelming.

I was back in the reception area when I heard a noise from outside. My heart sent a lightning jolt through my body as fear set in. Footsteps. I crouched down to hide near the window, and I held my breath as I peered over the windowsill and looked to the street. It was broad daylight, the sun beat down on the street, light reflecting off each object. I listened carefully, trying to spot anything, anyone moving around. I could hear the footsteps getting closer, they weren't trying to be quiet by any means, just simply strolling through the city. To my left, out of the corner of my eye, I saw where the noise was coming from.

A person came into view. A young man. He wore head to toe black combat gear. A large weapon slung across his back, over the top of a backpack and he had an army knife strapped around his leg. His black boots were laced to the top tightly and his jacket was covered in pockets. The backpack was large, the kind you would take hiking and fill with all the necessary things. The sun bounced off his curly hair, making the black mess appear almost purple in the light. He was just wandering the street, quietly humming to himself. It seemed as though he didn't have a care in the world.

*Maybe this wasn't such a waste of time after all,* I thought, and raised my eyebrow in intrigue.

I watched him as he strode past, kicking some of the rubbish and peering downward as if to look at something before continuing on. He hummed a beautiful, slow tune. It was a low hum and sounded like a sad song. One that would bring you to tears if you knew the meaning.

I was careful to squeeze back out of the window, trying not to make a noise and let the mystery man know I was watching him. Once he was a healthy distance away, I began to follow him. I was much better at being quiet than he was, so I was sure he wouldn't know I was trailing him.

He walked for some time, only stopping every now and then to observe a piece of litter, a bin or sometimes a carcass. He ducked into a building and was out of sight for about ten minutes, before appearing again. He walked with such confidence I questioned if it were I who was being ridiculous by spending my days sneaking around. Nothing came out of the shadows to devour him, hunt him or snatch him, even as he was being overtly loud. He sat down on a ruined bench that would've once been a bus stop and gazed into the distance. I was so confused as to why he was acting as though everything was normal. He seemed completely unfazed by the chaos surrounding him.

"Are you going to follow me until the sun goes down?" He said calmly, his voice not faltering. I froze and said nothing, staying behind the building as I held my breath. I was contemplating running away when he spoke again. "I'm not going to hurt you. You can come out." He turned to face my direction. He crossed his foot over his opposite knee and casually waited. I sheepishly rounded the corner, slowly moving into his view.

"Ah, see. That wasn't so hard." He grinned and leaned back. One arm draped over the bench to get a better look at me. He couldn't be much older than me, maybe in his early twenties. And he was beautiful, in a very dark and mysterious way. "Why are you following me?" He asked.

I kept quiet, not moving any closer to him. I stared at him with obvious confusion on my face. You couldn't trust anyone anymore, strangers, neighbours, friends had all become blind with fear. I gripped my weapon tightly to remind myself where it was and that I had the power to use it if I needed.

He had an athletic build and even sitting down, I could tell that he was tall. His hair was well kept, even if it was a curly mess on top of his head. He was well groomed and clean. His eyes were a deep brown, but behind the shadow of his brow, they could have been black. With sharp facial features, he was stunning. He didn't look tired and exhausted as I did. His clothes looked like they were the real deal. I wondered if he was part of the army or maybe he was a Snatcher. No, Snatchers weren't this put together.

He looked at me expectantly. "Okay. Let's start with something easy then. What is your name?"

I took two steps closer to him and replied cautiously, "Who are you?" My body was tense and I was ready to run at any point.

"I'm Luke." He held out his hand waiting for me to shake it. I did not.

"Melody." I replied without moving forward to reciprocate his gesture.

"Melody." He repeated. "It's nice to meet you." He retracted his hand and shrugged off the rejection. "Why are you following me?"

"I wasn't following you." I snapped back, heat rushing to my cheeks.

"Oh, okay. So, you just happened to be walking the same direction as me?" He tilted his head back slightly as he laughed. His arrogance was annoying.

"Luke, is it?" I paused, "Why are you walking around here making so much noise?" I whispered, waving my hand around to the surrounding buildings making a point to keep my voice low.

He looked outright offended. "I don't need to be quiet." He slouched back into the bench. I scoffed loudly and he smiled at me. His eyes were menacing and dark.

The sunlight reflected off something hanging around his neck. When my eyes found his pendant, he gently grasped it and tucked it back into his shirt.

"Why are you walking the streets of the city alone, Melody?" His voice lowered as he sounded my name. A shiver rushed through my body and I became very aware that I was alone and no one knew where I was.

*Could I fight this man off? Could I run faster than him?* I thought to myself.

"I am no threat to you. You don't need to worry." He waved his hand through the air casually. It was as if he had read my thoughts. He was so relaxed that it only made me more tense.

"Are you with the Army?" I asked.

"No." His response was quick and flat.

"Snatchers?" I spat out.

"Definitely not." He laughed.

I didn't reply, but I kept my eyes locked on him. A million questions passed through my mind.

"Anyway, it was lovely meeting you and having this..." He paused and gestured with his hands as he stood from the bench, "...conversation. But I must be getting back." He brushed invisible dust from his pants and walked towards me. He stopped, shoulder to shoulder with me and my whole body straightened, heart pounding in my chest as he leaned into my ear and spoke softly, "I hope to see you again soon, Melody." And he strode off, with the same confidence and humming as before.

I stood watching him for a moment as he walked into the distance. That was the first person I had spoken to, except my mother and brother, in a long time. I had seen people in the streets, here and there. But everyone was the same, scared, hurried, and not stopping for another person in case that ended up being the last thing they did. These past few months, I hadn't seen anyone.

I walked towards home as the sun began to set. I hoped Daniel would be home before me, so I could tell him of my encounter.

I couldn't stop thinking about Luke. He was so careless about being quiet, his arrogance at the forefront of my mind, irritating me. Irritating me probably more than it should have. I wondered how he has been getting around the city being so loud and reckless. I didn't want to try it myself and risk meeting my end, so I kept to my usual sneaking, stepping carefully and not making a sound as I made my way back through the city.

# Chapter 3

I had wandered further from home than I realised. I must have lost track of the streets when I was trailing Luke. I still had some time before I was home, so I picked up the pace, the air became cool and the sun dipped below the buildings.

I heard an intense growl, stopping me in my tracks. My body froze, I backed myself into the nearest building and clasped my spear to my chest with both hands. My heart quickened, throbbing through my veins and ears as my body stilled. I looked around carefully, trying to see where the horrible noise came from. I didn't need to see it to know exactly what it was. I could hear heavy footsteps crunching around the corner. They were slow, intentional steps. Not trying to go undetected, but quiet as if they were listening, listening for me.

I held my breath and slowly peered around the corner. There it was. A creature. One that was so far from humanity that it could no longer shift back. Its dark grey, almost black skin looked like leather with long gangly arms that had been slightly distorted during its final shift. It walked hunched over, on all fours, reminding me of a gorilla. It was a hairless beast, horrible to look at. A large overgrown head sat on top of a slender neck. Its jaw gaped open to reveal an overcrowded mouth, full of razor-sharp teeth. Old blood dried around its lips and saliva dripped in sticky beads from its mouth. I gulped hard when I saw its eyes, they were so human, the only traces that it was ever a different form. Greenish-blue eyes darted around as it sniffed the air, looking for me. It was unsettling, how a creature so horrid could have such human eyes. I wondered if there was a soul trapped inside. Screaming to get out, with no control of the beast that now owned its body. As it walked the streets leaving nothing but carnage in its tracks.

I leaned back into the building, there was nowhere for me to hide, it was coming my direction, and I was stuck in the open. With only my makeshift spear to help me. I took a deep breath and felt my stomach twist as I realised, I would either have to risk running or fight it, both scenarios had a high chance of me becoming the creature's next meal. I chose the latter. I would rather die trying, than die fleeing.

Gripping my spear, I sucked in a deep breath and closed my eyes. Preparing to step out into the creature's line of vision.

A hand grabbed my shoulder firmly, and I jumped with fright, swinging around. Luke stood there, grasping me tight, index finger to his lips.

"Shh." He whispered and motioned for me to follow him.

I did so without question. I would much rather face Luke than the creature. He pulled me behind him in protection, and we slowly walked backwards, in the opposite direction from the creature. Contrary to earlier, Luke was careful with his steps, keeping them light and without sound.

The creature rounded the corner just as Luke and I ducked low behind an old post box that had been turned on its side. He kept one arm gripped tightly around my own. Making sure to keep himself between the creature and me. The creature rose up on its legs to sniff high into the sky and came down with all its weight. The impact rumbled through the ground. During its mutation, it had become much bigger than an adult man. Its distorted muscles and body parts weighed it down heavily.

Luke turned to me, his dark brown eyes locking with mine and whispered, "Stay here, be quiet and do not do anything stupid." His nose was almost touching mine. I nodded in understanding.

My heart was racing so fast, I wanted to run but I did as I was told and crouched lower behind the box. Luke dropped his bag, unlaced his boots and kicked them off, then removed his black jacket and dropped it at my feet. I didn't have time to question him before he stood up from behind the post box and walked out of view, towards the creature. I heard a deep groaning noise, then sounds of flesh tearing and bone snapping. Luke made a pained noise and I almost peaked around the box to see what was happening, but I knew the creature had spotted him. As a low snarl came from the pit of its stomach and its steps came bounding towards him. I closed my eyes and cupped my hands over my ears as they collided. I expected to hear Luke screaming as it devoured him, but all I heard were the growls and snarls of animals fighting. Like I had the nature channel on. I couldn't resist anymore and gazed around the side of the post box. I couldn't believe what I was seeing.

Two creatures were going head-to-head. The one I had spotted before was being tackled and thrown around like a ragdoll. The other creature was different, a lighter shade of grey, almost glistening in the evening light and it stood on its legs instead of the animalistic way the former walked. The new creature moved swiftly on its feet as if it weighed nothing at all. Using its strength and agility to run circles around the dark grey creature. The dark grey one was rabid, moving without thought and stumbling over its overgrown limbs. It slashed its claws through the air carelessly. One of the blows sliced through the chest of the light grey creature. The beast stepped back and cried out loudly before lunging forward again. The match was short lived when the lighter creature plummeted the first one into the ground and stood over it. The creature on the ground, still trying to fight be-tween laboured breaths, clawed aimlessly at the beast on top of it. The lighter one placed both its hands on either side of its head and snapped its neck in a sudden, sharp movement.

The creature on the ground fell limp.

It was dead.

The second creature turned to face my direction, and I scurried back behind the post box, heart pounding in my ears. I could hear it making its way towards me, I fumbled for my spear, but when I grabbed it and straightened, I was face to face with the creature. My heart felt like it stopped working, the whole world moved in slow motion for only a moment.

Dark brown eyes stared back at me. Luke's eyes.

I gasped as I tried to make sense of what I had just seen. The creature stared straight into my eyes, letting out a deep exhale. He was wounded, a large gash on his chest dripping fresh crimson blood. I couldn't move, my body was stiff with fear and confusion. His body began to violently shake, his eyes closing to bear the pain. He pushed his head into my chest, and I instinctively wrapped my arms around him, completely shocked by what was happening. I held onto his shoulders as he shook uncontrollably, his body morphing before my eyes. He was shifting. He clenched his teeth, panting and all I could do was sit and watch as his body contorted. He pressed into my chest further, needing the comfort of my touch, of my arms around him. His long grey arms bent and snapped back into place, and I winced with every sharp noise. His skin started bubbling and changing colour as the bones and muscles moved underneath. His panting quickened as his body took a human form. Sweat trailing down his shoulders and onto the pavement. I couldn't take my eyes off him.

After a moment, it was over, and he was laying in my lap, naked.

He looked up at me and spoke through gritted teeth, "Shelter. We need shelter." I understood what he meant. It was too late for us to be travelling, and we would be spending the night out in the open. I wrapped his arm around my neck and helped him to stand. I swung his bag over my shoulder and helped him get his jacket and boots on. It didn't offer him much modesty, but it would have to do for now.

I decided to go back to the medical centre I had explored earlier. Squeezing through the broken window again and setting up in the staff room. I found some navy-blue scrubs in one of the cupboards and gave him the pants first. He pulled them up quickly and winced at the movement. He sat down on the ground and leaned his back against the wall, taking steadying breaths. I went to look for something to help with his bleeding wound.

This was a medical centre, surely they had medical supplies.

I walked to the end of the corridor and tried the door again. I held the handle tightly and shoved my body against the door, hard. I hissed at the pain that shot through my shoulder. I tried again and again, not making a dent in the door at all.

"My turn?" Luke said standing behind me.

I moved to the side and with one swift motion, he broke the door down and tumbled through the threshold. My eyes widened as I stepped through and took in the small room. It was a medical supply cupboard, filled with medicine, bandages and other things.

"Jackpot." I said and began to fill my bag with anything that would fit.

Luke followed me back to the staffroom and I pulled out a chair for him. "Here, sit down. Let me see your wound."

He stood in the doorway and smiled at me. I looked at him as he took his bloodied jacket off carefully, dropping it to the ground. I stared in disbelief when I saw his chest. The gaping wound that was bleeding before was now closed with a dark pink scar forming. I moved to him quickly and examined the scar. He watched me intensely as I traced the scar with gentle fingers, from his right collar bone, across his chest and stopping just over his left ribs.

"W-what..." I stuttered.

"It's been a while since I've had to do that." He saw the question on my face because he quickly added, "Quick healing. It's definitely a perk of shifting." He grabbed the scrub shirt and pulled it over his head carefully.

"Are you okay?" I asked. Still gawking at his healed wound.

"Yeah, just a bit tender." He laughed and walked over to the table and motioned for me to sit in the chair I had pulled out for him.

There were too many thoughts running through my head that I couldn't put into words. I slumped into the chair silently and sipped from one of my water bottles. Luke sat opposite me and gulped down the water bottle I offered him.

"What just happened?" I finally asked.

"I saved your ass, that's what." He was leaning back in his chair with his cool demeanour again. As if what just happened was part of his usual daily routine.

I stared at him without blinking, "You're not going to explain what the hell just happened?" I retorted.

I was more confused than ever at what I had just witnessed. He had shifted on command and been conscious enough to follow through with what he wanted and then shift back. I never had any control over my shifting and never remembered what happened.

"So many questions, Melody." He purred my name out. "You could just say thank you and be done with it." I said nothing, waiting for him to explain. "Okay, okay. What do you want to know?" he leaned forward.

"How can you do that, shift on command?"

He reached into his shirt and pulled out the pendant I had seen earlier. It was a perfect circle, like a silver coin, only it was as big as a golf ball. It was engraved with intricate lines and details, in the centre of it was a dark black stone. "I was given this pendant. It helps me channel my energy, so I can control it. I shift when I want to, shift back when I want to."

"What is it?" I asked, leaning forward to see it better.

"The stone is black tourmaline. I am not really sure how it works. But the stone helps to channel energy and with training it helps to gain control over shifting."

"So, you have complete control over it?" I asked.

"Yeah, more or less. I was taught how to control it. I don't shift very much anymore because it's pretty intense, as you saw." He rolled his shoulders backwards, stretching.

"How did you get the pendent?" I asked eagerly.

"Back in the war, I was in one of the troops on the front-line. My troop was there when the explosion happened. The explosion was a mistake. There was some sort of chemical reaction. It all happened so quickly," He blinked away the memory, and I could've sworn I saw something like guilt flash across his face before he continued, "Only six of us made it out and when we were taken back to base. The medical team realised there was something really wrong with us. So, the General ordered us to be taken somewhere else. That was before the lab. Before anyone shifted. Then once more people started mutating, they needed to secure all of us and took us underground, creating the lab." He stood up and circled around the room, "Do you know anything about the lab, Melody?"

I shook my head, utterly silent as he continued.

"Well, it's not a nice place. I was there for months. They took so many vials of my blood, I thought I'd pass out. They kept us all separate and we were chained to our beds. We were put through *tests*. Extreme tests. As time went on, the test became more brutal. They told us they were searching for a cure, going to save us. But that wasn't what they were doing at all. They were torturing us to get us to shift back and forth between forms. Collecting as much data and information about the creatures and the shifting as they could. I don't remember much, because I was so drugged up and out of it. From the six of us, only two survived."

"How did you get out?" I asked, almost a whisper.

"One of the doctors, Greg Osbourn, was the second in charge and I think he realised something else was going on. Something dark. His superior, Dr Gelch was running the whole sadistic thing. Osbourn risked everything to get us out, myself and Oscar. I haven't seen him since. I owe him my life" He leant against the door frame with his arms crossed, eyes wide as he relived those memories.

"So, who gave you the pendent?"

"Oh, yeah." He held onto the pendent again, "Oscar and I stayed together for some time. We found an abandoned building and hid there for about one week. But one night, after Oscar shifted, he didn't come back. I assumed he had been caught by those assholes, the Snatchers, and taken back to the lab. I decided it was best to get out of the city. When I made it to the forest, I ran into an old friend from the army, Tobias. He had been affected too, after the explosion. He told me of this place, Illumina. It's a safe haven for people like me. People who shift. That's where he taught me to control it and where I was given the pendent."

"Illumina." I repeated. There was a safe haven. Illumina. My heart almost did a backflip in my chest. I needed to find this place. I needed to get there before Snatchers found me or before I shifted permanently.

The moon was high in the sky and my eyelids were heavy with exhaustion. I laid down on the ground, using my backpack as a pillow. Luke found a clear spot on the other side of the room and lay down.

"Thank you." I said, "For saving me." And I drifted off into a dreamless sleep.

~~~
~~~

I woke hours later, the morning light beginning to creep through the building. Luke was fast asleep on the other side of the room. He was laying on his side, his head resting on top of his arm and he was lightly snoring. I watched him for a moment, studying his face. His long black lashes resting atop his cheeks.

I remembered his toned, shirtless body I saw last night and warmth flushed my cheeks. I turned away quickly and sat up, trying to erase the thought from my mind.

He stirred awake and made a low groan as he stretched and rolled onto his back.

"Good morning sunshine." His voice was sleepy, and he barely opened his eyes.

I didn't reply to him as I stood and stretched my arms over my head. I turned to face Luke, who was still laying on his back, resting on his arms that were now folded behind his head. He looked striking, he kept his eyes fixed on me.

"I need you to take me to Illumina, the safe haven you told me about last night." I said, more of a demand.

"Why?" He didn't move his body at all.

"Because I need help." I replied, a lump forming in my throat. "I shift too. It's been happening for months." I almost burst into tears. The first admission out loud.

He didn't say anything for a moment, just sat up on his elbows. My eyes wandered down his chest, where his scrub shirt had bunched up a little and the lower part of his stomach was showing.

"I see." He said, snapping my attention back to his face. "Then we better get out of the city."

He explained briefly how to get to Illumina and that it would take us over a week on foot. "It's not an easy trip." He explained, "It's dangerous in the forest."

I told him I wanted to bring my family, and he reluctantly agreed to come to my house to try to speak to them. He said it was dangerous to involve other people, but I couldn't leave them behind.

We spoke scarcely as we walked through the city, trying not to make unnecessary noise and creep through unnoticed. Luke was more than happy to humour me and keep the humming to a minimum.

"It's a beautiful tune." I said quietly.

"My mother used to sing to me when I was a baby. It's the only thing I remember about her." I could sense the hesitation in his voice, so I chose not to probe further.

We came into my neighbourhood and the air felt less dense, allowing us to relax a little. The midmorning sun was warming everything around us. I tilted my head towards the sky and basked in it for a moment.

"So, Melody, tell me a bit about yourself." Luke said, snapping me back to reality, as we walked through the streets.

"There's not much to tell." I shrugged.

"I'm sure there is. What were you doing before the war broke out?" He smiled over his shoulder at me.

"I just finished school and got accepted into two universities. But I was going to take a year off. Maybe do some volunteer work." I hadn't decided which Uni I wanted to go to, so taking a year off sounded like a good idea at the time. It gave me more time to decide what I wanted to do.

"What were you going to Uni for?"

"To be a doctor." Luke raised his eyebrows, so I quickly added. "My dad was a doctor."

"You're really smart then?" He nudged me and I blushed again.

"I suppose." We laughed.

I told Luke about my regular childhood, my family and what had happened to my father. He told me about his family, or lack thereof.

"My mother left when I was about four years old. I didn't have brothers or sisters, and my dad wasn't the nurturing type. So, I followed in his footsteps and joined the army." He paused as if he was trying to push down whatever feeling was rising. "I didn't hear from him once I got drafted, because of the war and then everything that followed. I have no idea if he's alive."

I stopped walking and placed my hand on his arm. "I'm sorry." I said.

"For what?" He laughed and pulled his arm away. "It's fine, I made a family in the army. Which way?" He gestured between two streets and waited for me to direct him. I pointed to the left and we rounded the corner towards my house.

We entered through the front door. And as expected, my mother was in her room and Daniel was nowhere to be found. After Luke changed into spare clothes he had in his backpack, I gave him a very idle tour of the house. Avoiding my mother's room altogether. Then I took him into the backyard.

Our yard was small. Only big enough for a small garden shed in the back left corner, an even smaller vegetable patch and the apple tree towards the right. We had a little table and two chairs set up under the veranda. Luke and I chose to sit on them and enjoy an apple each.

"Thanks for the apple." He said taking another bite, the juices dripping down the side of his mouth. "It's been a while since I've had something so fresh."

We talked for hours, watching the sun move across the sky. Luke was not only confident, but he was also very charming and charismatic. He was so easy to talk to, it felt like I had known him longer than just a day. He spoke so highly of his friends before the war, naming more names than I could remember. But he spoke with deep sorrow for his friend Oscar. The guilt he felt for not going back to look for him. He told me many stories of his time in the army and how it shaped him into who he was now. From the lonely childhood he had, to finding a family in his friends. He didn't speak of much that happened during the war or after the explosion. The memories seemed too painful to bring up again.

I had much less to say than him. We talked about what our futures used to look like, and it all seemed so silly now, a life that would never be.

The back door swung open and Daniel came out. He glanced between Luke and I before snapping, "Bringing strays home now?"

# Chapter 4

Daniel sat stoned faced on the couch in the living room as Luke and I explained everything. I told him everything I could remember, sparing no details. About my shifting, when it started, the nightmares and the creature that Luke and I encountered in the city. Luke spoke about Illumina, the safe haven, and that we needed to find it. I practically begged Daniel to come with us. Still, he sat there without saying a word. His elbows rest on his knees and his fingers interlaced.

"Okay." He finally said.

"Okay?" I repeated as a question.

"Yeah, it's not like I have anything else to do. Plus, I'd rather die out there in the action than in that damned basement." He motioned to the basement door with his head.

"Great, we leave in the morning. Pack light, just bring the necessities." Luke said. "Bring some weapons, it'll be dangerous." Daniel grinned at that comment.

I stood from the couch, "I'll go tell…"

As I turned to face the kitchen, I saw our mother standing there, one hand on her heart and the other stabilising herself on the kitchen countertop, her eyes were wide like she'd seen a ghost.

"No." She rasped, almost a whisper.

"Let me explain…" I replied.

"I said no!" She tried to shout at me, "Those *things* took your father from me, and you invited one into this house. *His* house?" She clasped her shirt tightly, pointing at Luke with her other hand. "How dare you." She was breathless.

"There is a place that will keep us safe." I slowly stalked towards her, scared if I moved quickly, she would retreat to her room. "I need to go, I need help." I said as a whisper.

"Get out!" she yelled at Luke, "Get out you vile *creature!*" She waved her slender finger towards Luke, who was already making his way quickly towards our back door. Avoiding eye contact with her.

My mother collapsed to her knees. She was so weak that even this conversation was enough to overwhelm her. I rushed to her side, swinging my arm around her waist and the other stabilising her hand. I helped her to stand and took her back to her bedroom where I left her sitting on the edge of her bed, murmuring something about my father. Even if she was in agreement to come to Illumina, she would never make it out of the city.

No one was in the lounge room when I came back to the room. I passed the kitchen and went through the back door, outside. Daniel and Luke were standing under the veranda, both with their arms crossed speaking quietly. They were the same height though Daniel had golden, straight hair and light hazel eyes and Luke, with his black curly hair and deep brown eyes. They were like night and day.

"Luke, I'm really sorry." I came to stand with them. "She hasn't been the same since..."

"You don't need to apologise." He cut me off. "The war has changed everything. It's fine." He placed his hand on my shoulder and gave me an endearing look. I didn't need his pity, after all, we have all suffered.

"Let's just get inside, pack some things and get some rest." Daniel said as he turned to walk inside. "Beans for dinner."

After dinner I made Luke a pitiful bed on our two-seater couch and handed him a blanket. "It's comfier than it looks." I shrugged.

"Better than some places I've slept." He smiled at me, showing off his perfect white teeth. My cheeks heated and I quickly looked away before he noticed. I turned to walk down the hallway.

"Goodnight, Melody." The way Luke said my name made me weak at the knees.

"Goodnight Luke." I called back. Daniel was leaning against his bedroom door frame directly opposite my room. His eyebrows raised high in an accusatory way.

"What?" I quietly snapped at him.

Daniel rolled his eyes at me and disappeared into the darkness of his room. I slipped into my bedroom and packed a few spare clothes, and other things I thought I might need into my biggest backpack. Making sure the medical supplies were packed too. I felt like a kid before Christmas morning, I hopped into bed excited to do something new tomorrow. Get out of the city, go find Illumina. It didn't take long for sleep to sweep over me.

~~~

*I dug my claws deep into the dirt. Feeling the vibrations of the footsteps surrounding me. I was hidden in the shadows, and the new senses that overcame my body gave me a clear advantage over them. My body felt strong, stronger than it ever had before. I could hear the voices of people yelling commands to one another. I was being hunted. The Snatchers were closing in, and they had no idea that I was about to rip them to shreds like it was nothing. Two men dressed head to toe in fighting leathers came around the corner, weapons steady in their hands. They took careful footsteps in my direction, although I knew they hadn't seen me yet. My heart slowed to an almost stop, I waited until they were close and then lunged. Red filled my vision, they screamed and more Snatchers came rushing towards me. Towards their death.*

I sat up in my bed and held my hand over my heart. It was racing. My sheet was covered in sweat. Another sleep, ruined by my ongoing nightmares. I shook my head to try to dull the vision that still stung behind my eyes. The vision of me, tearing apart the Snatchers.

I lay back down and tried to get comfortable again. It was still night, and I needed to try to rest before setting off in the morning. As I tossed and turned trying to quiet my mind, my eyes shot open at a loud bang that shook the house.
~~~

Daniel, Luke and I got up quickly and gathered in the lounge room.

"What was that?" Luke asked quietly.

"No idea, it sounded close though." Daniel went over to the window to listen again.

Another loud bang sounded even closer this time, causing the glassware to rattle. My arms shot out to grab onto something to try to stabilise myself and my hand found Lukes. I grasped his hand tightly.

"That was way closer!" I shouted. I looked towards the hallway, to where our mothers' room was and ran to get her.

I went quickly down the hall and swung open her bedroom door. When I was at the foot of her bed, I grabbed the bedsheet and pulled it back. She was gone.

I ran to the bathroom, searching for her. I shouted for her in each doorway.

"What's wrong Mel?" Daniel called from the lounge.

I joined them around the couch, panting from panic. "She's gone." Was all I said before I ran off again to search the house. Daniel and Luke followed and looked all over the house once more, just to be sure. But there was no sign of our mother. No sign of her leaving either.

"She must have left." Said Luke.

"You don't understand, she wouldn't just leave!" I said through my teeth.

"Well, she isn't here." Luke replied.

"She must have left before the shutters went down." Daniel said, almost a whisper.

Before I could argue with him, an enormous explosion came through the front of the house and into our dining area. I was knocked off my feet and thrown across the room with the power of it. My chest was throbbing and my ears were ringing. My vision was blurred and when I tried to look around the room, I saw rubble and dust. It took me a moment to realise what had just happened. I grabbed my head and tried to steady my vision.

"Daniel?" I coughed as I struggled to my feet. I was off balance and fell back down, grasping my head again.

"Here." A sound rasped from under the debris. Daniel was lying face down, with crushed bits of our house on top of him. I crawled over to him quickly and hurried to get him out.

"Daniel, are you okay?" My hands tore through the debris to get to him.

He coughed and rose to his hands and knees, nodding slightly to confirm he wasn't badly hurt. My heart skipped a beat in relief. There was movement in the corner of my eye and Luke appeared, also buried under the aftermath of the explosion, but not hurt.

We heard voices yelling coming from outside the house. We had been ambushed.

"Quick! They're in there! They're in there!" A woman said loudly. Her voice was too familiar. "Get them!" She yelled.

Without a word, the three of us huddled together, we grabbed our backpacks and weapons and slipped out the back door.

I stopped to look back but Daniel grabbed my arm and tugged softly. "Mel, we need to go now!" He yelled.

I followed him without argument, and we ran through the backyard, escaping over the fence. We ran down the street, keeping to the shadows to avoid the Snatchers on the street. We stopped out of sight and looked back towards the disaster that we had left behind. The Snatchers had surrounded our house and leaked out through the neighbouring streets when they realised we had escaped.

Then I saw her. Our mother, walking with the Snatchers through our backyard. A whimper escaped my body, and I clasped my hand over my mouth. She was going to hand us over to them. My heart broke into pieces as I watched her. Luke placed his hand on my back and I realised that I was crying.

"W-Why would she do that?" I sobbed, not looking for a reply. I buried my face into Luke's broad chest and he held me tightly as I sobbed.

After a short moment of silence, we turned in the opposite direction and started to walk quickly towards the forest. I glanced back at our childhood home, now destroyed in more ways than one. The sky was beginning to shine a beautiful orange as the sun tried to peep over the horizon. I wiped tears from my cheek and straightened my back; I looked down at the house, chin high, I hoped I would never see that house again.

We walked through the neighbourhood quickly, towards the edge where it met the forest. We kept our footsteps quick and quiet, as the Snatchers now swarmed the streets. They were out for blood, our blood.

"Two more streets over and we will be at the edge of the forest." Daniel pointed in front of us as we crouched below an overgrown hedge. "Then we run like hell."

We were careful and quiet and made it to the forest in no time at all. As we moved into the brush, our steps quickened into a sprint, putting as much space between us and the Snatchers as we could. When we were all panting and in need of a quick break, we stopped. Each of us searching for a water bottle to replenish ourselves.

"They will be after us now." Luke said as he sipped at his water. He leaned up against a tree casually.

I sat down near him and angled my head to look up at him. "What do you mean?" I said between my laboured breaths.

"We've been 'tagged' now. Made known to them. So, they're going to keep coming for us." He explained.

"Great! Another thing to look forward to." Daniel threw his hands in the air.

"Don't worry, I was tagged a long time ago and they haven't caught me yet." Luke laughed.

Neither Daniel nor I laughed. I looked around the forest, it was beautiful. Tall trees reaching high into the sky. With sunlight shining through, making yellow and orange dapples across the forest floor. Some birds were singing in the treetops, and I wondered how they could still be so cheerful after everything that had happened. I hadn't ventured into the forest since the beginning of everything. I was too scared too, especially when we heard of the animals mutating too.

"It'll add a bit of fun to our trip. Don't you think so?" Luke said light heartedly.

"Great." I said dully.

"Great." Daniel repeated.

We sat for a short moment, to catch our breath. Then we were off again. We decided to keep a quick pace but not run to preserve our energy for the long journey ahead. We wanted as much space between us and the Snatchers as possible, and anything else that was out there.

"Our best bet for making it through the night is to climb high in the trees and rest there." Luke said as we walked. "There are things in the forest that would be best to avoid." We had been walking for hours, only stopping briefly to rest and drink or eat.

"Up in the trees?" I asked, looking up the length of the tree in front of me. It was enormous, I doubted if I could climb that high.

"Yes, we don't want to be caught on the ground by anything out here." Luke replied with a low voice. The air was cooling as the sun was starting to dip behind the mountains in the distance. "Let's stop here, eat something and then get into the trees." Luke said. He was more on edge out here than I had seen him in the city. I wondered what he had experienced during his first journey to Illumina, but I didn't have the guts to ask him.

"Okay Boss. Which tree?" Daniel said jokingly.

"I think we should spread out and each be in our own tree." Luke gazed upward and I noticed the vein in his neck pulsing. His heart was beating quickly, which made me nervous.

"Wouldn't we be safer together?" I asked, shyly.

"Our scents will be stronger if we're together." Luke stared deep into my eyes, and my cheeks grew hot. "Last time I was out here, it was just me. And I didn't run into too much trouble." He shrugged.

Thankfully, the weather was still warm enough during the night that we wouldn't be freezing. Still, the thought of sleeping in a tree was not appealing to me at all. When we finished our tinned dinners, Luke picked a tree each for us. Then he gave orders on how far apart we needed to be.

"Melody, you take this one. Daniel, you up that one and I'll be here." He had placed us in a triangle shape. Saying it would be easier to keep an eye on each other that way.

I stood at the base of my tree and bent my neck backwards to observe the climb I had ahead of me. I gulped hard and looked over my shoulder towards Luke. He met my eyes and winked as he scaled up his tree with ease. Daniel and I began our ascent. He was much quicker than me, hauling himself up each branch.

I reached up to the branches, holding on tightly as I pulled myself up. Each foot placement was carefully considered, and sometimes I lost my footing and slipped. I tried to imagine I was climbing a very strange ladder, not daring to look down. I frowned with concentration as I looked at each branch I was going to grasp.

I finally made it high enough to stop and get into a comfortable position. I straddled the large branch and faced towards the tree, hugging it tightly. I looked towards Daniel, who was sitting awkwardly on his branch, fidgeting around uncomfortably. I held in my laugh and my eyes wandered over to Luke. He had opted for a much more casual position. Leaning with his back towards the tree and legs crossed over one another. He had clearly done this before. He placed a glove over his eyes to cover them and tilted his head back slightly. He may have already fallen asleep. I settled in and tried to close my eyes.

The sun was disappearing quickly, and I knew we had a long night ahead of us.

# Chapter 5

The moon was hidden behind the clouds, making it darker than usual. I tried to get to sleep but whenever I felt like I was drifting away, I was brought back to reality with the strange noises of the forest. Leaves crunching below us, trees swaying and groaning in the cool night breeze.

Some animals came right under us, though it was too dark, and we were too high to see them. I was hoping that meant they couldn't see us either. Or smell us. The night felt long, it dragged on as I was constantly drifting in and out of sleep. I tried to eye Daniel and Luke a few times, but it was too hard to see them through the shadows.

Just as I drifted off again, I was startled awake by a low snarl. I gripped the tree tightly as my eyes darted around in search of where the sound came from. I could hear that Daniel was also alert and moving on his branch. Luke was silent. The leaves below us crunched and twigs and branches were snapped as the animal moved around. It sounded large.

I could hear each of its deep and loud breaths. I desperately tried to see Daniel or Luke, to make eye contact with one of them, or see if I could make my way over to them through the treetops. My heart pounded wildly and vibrated through my ears. The snarl came again, only this time it was more primal. Every hair on my body rose as goosebumps covered my skin. The sound wasn't a normal growl. It had an unearthly sound to it.

Something monstrous.

I shuffled around on my branch to try to see the animal. Panic set in as I realised how unprotected we were. My breaths quickened and I felt lightheaded. I held a hand to my chest and my fingers tried to claw their way in, to try steady my heart. Then I felt a solid hand grip my shoulder, I turned quickly to see Luke sat on the branch behind me. He had been so silent, that I hadn't noticed him moving through the treetops. I let out a breath of relief.

"Shh" He whispered into my ear and a chill ran up my spine. "It can't see us, but it can smell us."

"What is it?" I asked through my breath, heart pounding.

"I don't know yet, I haven't got a good look at it yet. But it's huge and it's been mutated from the radiation." His voice was low. He kept his hand on my shoulder, holding me tight and I leaned into him further.

My eyes searched the ground, we could still hear it walking around below. I could just make out Daniel's shape, as the clouds moved in the sky and the moonlight shone through. He was still sitting on the branch, his body tense as he surveyed the ground below. Luke was using his hands to motion to Daniel to try and get across to us. But Daniel just stared back blankly and threw his hands up in the air, mouthing some sort of profanity. Either, he had no idea what Luke was saying, or he thought it was a terrible idea. Either way, he wasn't moving.

"We need to get over to Daniel. Looks like we might be safer together after all." Luke whispered, nudging me.

I rolled my eyes and nodded. "I think someone may have mentioned that earlier." I teased back.

Luke turned and stood on the branch swiftly. Holding both arms out to balance, he silently walked the branch like a plank. He made it look so easy. Slowing as the branch thinned out, he lined up a branch jutting out of the closest tree next to us. Then with a swift motion, he leaped onto the other branch. He was out of his mind if he thought I could do that. Once stable, he swivelled around to face me. He waved his hands, motioning for me to follow. My throat tightened and I swallowed hard. Now was not the time to chicken out. I turned on the branch, careful not to make any noise or drop my bag as I slung it over my shoulder. I slowly stood on the branch and held my arms out to help me balance. I was glad of how dark it was, it made it hard to tell how far away the ground was. I took a breath deep into my lungs and exhaled, meeting Luke's stare. His expression was tense, and he did not take his eyes off me as I took my first steps.

*One foot after the other. C'mon Melody, you can do this.* I told myself repeatedly. I closed the distance between Luke and I. And as I reached the jumping point, Luke reached his arms out, as if he was going to catch me. I held my arms out in return and jumped. My feet touched the branch first and I felt Luke's arms wrap around me, pulling me into his chest. He held me for a moment, and we both panted hard as we both remembered how to breathe again. With my ear to his chest, I could hear the steady beat of his heart.

"Not bad." Luke teased as he softened his grip on me but didn't let me go.

We repeated this until we were in the tree right next to Daniel. He watched us make our way closer, while also checking the ground continuously for danger. The forest was dimly lit by the moon now and we could see down to the forest floor. The three of us searched the ground to see if we could see the monster lurking below. But it seemed to have vanished. We all sat silently. I felt the warmth of Luke's body next to me and somehow, I felt safer.

"Where did it go?" Daniel said from across the tree. Luke shrugged but he hadn't let his guard down yet, keeping me on edge. Time went by, and we hadn't heard or seen anything again. None of us got any more sleep as the sun began to rise on the horizon. Once the forest was golden with the morning sun, we made our descent from the trees.

We walked all day, only stopping occasionally for food and rest. Luke was an average hunter. He said he had to figure it out when he left the city the first time. He was on his own then, I couldn't imagine facing this all alone. He was able to catch some rabbits and birds, mostly untouched by the radiation. The bigger the animals got, the more affected they seemed. We passed many dead animals, some killed and others seemed to have died from the mutations their bodies endured.

"Have either of you ever learned how to fight? Or defend yourselves?" Luke asked while we walked through the trees.

"No. I have never needed to know how." I said, a little embarrassed.

"Everyone should know the basics." Luke stopped walking and turned to face us. "What about you?" He said to Daniel, who shook his head. "Well, I'd better teach you a thing or two then. He dropped his bag against a tree and motioned for us to follow him.

Luke went over some moves that he called basic, although I struggled to pick them up. He was taller than me and obviously stronger, so had a clear advantage over me. "Use my height against me." He said, holding me tightly from behind. One arm wrapped around my neck and the other holding my head in place.

"I can't." I said, defeated.

"Just try." He explained different ways to get out of this hold, and when I managed it, he patted me on the back firmly.

I was proud of myself, even though I had a feeling he had let me go. He ran Daniel through the same moves and then told us to keep practicing on each other.

Two days went by, and we hadn't run into any danger. Though we stayed alert. We knew we were being hunted by the Snatchers and the sounds that rang throughout the forest were a constant reminder that we were not alone. We kept practicing the moves Luke had taught us whenever we had the chance and he threw in a few new moves each day.

"There should be a river over this hill." Luke said as he picked up the pace. "We can bathe and rest here for the night."

Daniel and I followed eagerly, it had been days since I had last washed. Even if it was going to be freezing, it was better than smelling like sweat and damp forest. We made it to the top of the hill and the river came into view. It was fast flowing and the riverbank was scattered with palm sized rocks. We would have to find a shallow spot to bathe if we didn't want to be dragged away by the current.

"Is it safe?" I asked.

"There is a little spot upstream, I think." Luke pointed.

We followed Luke further upstream and he was right. There was a shallow pool to the side of the flowing river. It was much safer than jumping straight into the current. The water eased through the shallow pool calmly and reflected light off the small ripples. I knelt next to the pool and felt the water. The sun had warmed it as it moved through the pool slowly. I sat down and pulled an apple from my bag, crunching into it.

Daniel stripped off to his underwear and waded into the water. It only came up to his knees, so he laid down and allowed the water to fully engulf him. When he resurfaced, he looked refreshed. His golden hair shone in the sunlight, and he smiled from ear to ear.

"I have never seen so much emotion on your face Dan." I said as I splashed him.

"I have never felt so free Mel. This is exactly what I needed." He splashed me back.

"You needed a war, a radioactive explosion, mutations and our mother betraying us so we would need to flee?" I asked him flatly. I teased, but the words still stung coming out.

"I needed to get out. There were things going on in the city that I... Never mind. I am just glad to be out. Things were changing, Mel." He replied.

"Not the only thing that was changing." I said, pointing towards myself.

Daniel scoffed and continued swimming around in the pool.

Luke joined me at the edge and nudged me. "Going in, Melody?" He asked.

I nodded but didn't move. I took another bite of my apple. Stalling. "Soon." I said. I didn't feel like taking off my clothes in front of them.

Luke flicked off his shoes and pulled his socks off, setting them down next to me. He pulled his shirt up over his head and my eyes couldn't help but wander down his chest. There was barely a scar where he was wounded the first time we met. I could only make it out if I looked hard. You would never know there was once a gaping wound there. My heart raced as my eyes followed his body downward. I blushed. He was toned, much more than I had expected. My eyes drifted all the way to his waistband, where his oblique muscles formed a V and dipped beneath his pants.

His pendant caught the sunlight and reflected in my eyes which broke my gaze.

I blinked repeatedly and looked around, thankfully no one had noticed me gawking at the sight of Luke shirtless. He pulled his pants off and followed Daniel into the water. I decided to take a walk around the river to see what I could find. Distract myself from the thoughts of Luke's half-naked body.

I slowly walked upstream, leaving Daniel and Luke to splash around in the shallow pool. The trees were tall and green reaching high into the sky. You would almost think it was beautiful. The grass danced with the wind and some small birds flew past in groups. Daniel and Luke were out of sight now, but I could still hear them when I came upon the body of a deer.

She was laying lifeless on the ground.

As I approached carefully, her legs began moving uncontrollably. The movement startled me, and I jumped back to watch her cautiously. Her legs moved back and forth, then stilled, letting out a low groan. I walked towards her quietly, and as I neared, I held my breath at the sight of her. She had not been hunted or killed. She was dying from mutations. Her legs were untouched by the radiation, but half her face was morphed into a bloodied mess. She had fungus-like lumps protruding from where her eye once was, it was moving with each of her laboured breaths. The larger lumps looked like they were on the verge of bursting, and some looked like they already had. Half her face had been eaten away by the mutation, and she was lying in a pool of her own fluids. She panted and groaned in pain. My heart broke and I wished I could end her suffering. But I just stood there and watched. She took her last breath moments later and her body finally stilled with the relief of death.

I walked back to the others sombrely and sat down with my bag.

"What's wrong with you?" Daniel asked, still swimming.

"Nothing." I snapped back. "I am just sick of this place." He knew not to push further and kept his distance from me for the rest of the afternoon.

I instantly felt guilty for snapping, knowing that Daniel could sense the tension on my face. He was always good at reading people and knowing when to push and when to back off. I gave him a single nod, which he returned when Luke told me that they were going to hunt for some dinner.

When the sun was setting and Daniel and Luke had left to find something to eat, I decided to stay back and finally wash. I stripped down to my underwear and I waded into the shallow pool, shuddering at the temperature. It was much colder than earlier today, but I didn't really mind. I held my breath as I fell below the water allowing it to rush over my body. I gasped as the cold washed over me, but I held myself underwater. Trying to numb my body and quiet my thoughts. I pushed myself back up, out of the water and took in a large breath. It felt nice to swim, to be weightless in the cool water. I floated on my back, staring at the sky and the dark clouds that were forming.

It was going to rain.

~~~
~~~

Daniel and Luke came back just as I had finished dressing. Luke was grinning in triumph as he held up two rabbits.

"Wow." I said monotone. "A meal fit for a king."

"Hey!" Luke said. "I'd like to see you do better."

"I'm just teasing." I said and forced out a laugh. "I appreciate not having to eat canned beans every night."

We finished eating and picked which tree to climb. We decided it was better to risk the animals smelling us and be in the same tree, than to be fending for ourselves in separate trees. Thunder rumbled over us and we knew there was a storm coming. The sky was a dark blue and grey as the clouds consumed any trace of the setting sun. The air was brisk and the wind blew hard, making the trees sway and groan.

The rain started off soft and light but soon began pelting down on us.

Hard.

It made it difficult to see as the water collided with us and ran down our faces, drenching us. I gripped the tree harder, and I could see that Luke was doing the same. Daniel was on the branch above us but if I looked up to him, I was sure my eyes would feel the full force of the raindrops. So, I faced down to the forest floor and squeezed my eyes shut, hoping to wait out the rain. Thunder cracked above us and we all jumped as lightning flashed in the sky. I was sure I saw something move in the distance.

Something large. A big black shadow was illuminated again with the lighting.

"Did you see that?" I yelled over the storm.

Luke shook his head but looked intensely to where I was pointing. Lightning flashed again and I knew we both saw the huge figure making its way towards us. Stalking closer. My heart was racing as I wiped the raindrops from my face and eyes, trying to clear my vision. I could feel Luke's body tense next to me and I dared to look up towards Daniel to warn him, but when I squinted up towards him, I knew he had already seen it.

I turned my head towards Luke. He must have read my expression because he placed his hands on my shoulder and took a deep breath, then put his index finger to his lips, telling me to stay quiet. He motioned for me to stay put while he climbed up to tell Daniel the same thing.

The rain was loud and pelted down on us, making it hard to see the figure as it moved towards us. I hoped that it wouldn't have been able to pick up our scent over the drenched forest floor. Being high in the tree gave us another advantage. We were all on edge with fear as it neared. With every flash of lightning the figure appeared closer and closer. When it was almost underneath us, Luke moved back down to my branch and huddled in close next to me. His presence was enough to take the edge off my nerves but didn't dull the pounding in my chest.

A crack of lightning hit the top of the tree, sending a shockwave through the centre of it.

I gripped the trunk harder as it snapped and split. Luke slipped back as the tree jolted and fell. Gravity took over and we were free falling. The tree collided with another, and

I was thrown from the branch in one brutal movement. Pain shot through my body as I broke the branches in my path.

I hadn't realised I was screaming until the wind was knocked out of me and I went silent.

Everything came to a halt, and I realised I had hit the forest floor. I clawed at my chest to try to draw in a breath, but I was winded. I rolled to my side and winced, recoiling as a sharp pain shot through my ribs. I blindly felt for where the pain came from and felt part of a branch lodged in my chest. I tried again to take in a breath and was able to draw in some air. My lunges were okay. I could feel my blood throbbing in my ears. My heartbeat was unsteady and too fast. Rain was still smashing down on my face as I lay on my back, trying to take in breaths, I could hear footsteps near me and turned my head to the side.

If I could have, I would have gasped, as the huge beast came into view. With the chaos of the fall, I had forgotten all about the animal stalking us. It was a bear, or it had been once. Now the huge animal stood taller than any bear should. Its body was mangled and had been mutated beyond anything I had seen. One of its front legs was grotesquely large for its already enormous body and dragged behind it. The muscles of its back were distorted into overgrown lumps. Its face was more reptilian than bear. Its lower jaw jutted out from its face and razor-sharp fangs as long as my forearm, filled its mouth. I watched the mutated bear walk slowly near me. Its face burying into the remains of the fallen trees, flipping them over one by one.

Daniel groaned from under the bear and it let out a loud growl as it found its prey.

"Daniel!" I tried to rasp out. But the pain in my chest made it sound more like a gurgle.

I couldn't let that thing get to my brother. I screamed in pain as I rolled over again.

My heart raced wildly. And I felt my bones crack and twist under my skin as I began to shift.

# Chapter 6

*I opened my eyes and saw the bear in front of me. Only, it looked smaller than it had before. My eyes darted to the body laying below it, he was still alive. The bear had noticed me and was charging. I ran full force towards it and as if in unison, lightning sounded as we collided. Limbs ripping at each other. The growls coming from the bear were loud. But mine were vicious. I slashed through its flesh. Chunks of its fur embedded under my talons.*

*I could not stop.*

*The bear tried again to attack me, but it was thrown back by my brute force. The animal now lay on its side snarling and spitting at me as I stood on top of it. With no thought I ripped into its body with my teeth, tearing the rest of it apart, bit by bit. Until there was nothing but blood and gore laying around me.*

*"That's enough." I heard a voice slide through my mind, not my own, but a familiar voice. I turned around to see another creature staring back at me. I recognised this creature. I had seen him be-*

*fore. He stared at me and his voice flowed through my mind again without his mouth moving.*

*"You need to stop now, be calm. Daniel is okay." The creature nodded his head towards the fallen trees, and the boy was now crouched behind them staring straight at me. Terror showing on his face. The creature moved towards me, and I took a step back, a defensive growl escaping my throat.*

*"It's okay Melody. Breath, slowly. You need to shift back." He took another few steps forward, closing the distance between us. His face was now directly in front of mine and I locked eyes with his. His beautiful dark eyes, so familiar. He took deep breaths and without realising, I mimicked his breathing, my heart beating slower and as I closed my eyes, the pain ripped through my body once more.*

~~~

I opened my eyes and my body ached all over. Each muscle felt as though it had been ripped off my bones and put back with rough force. I suppose they had. I tried to sit up, but I was held in place.

When I looked up, I saw Luke, with his arms wrapped tightly around me. He was asleep, but his expression was tense. I gently removed his arms, careful to not wake him and stood up. I looked down at my clothes, Luke's clothes. He must have dressed me after I shifted back to my human form.

I blushed at the thought of Luke seeing me naked.

I was wearing his black shirt that was too big and hung off my body and black cargo pants that matched his own.
~~~

Luckily there was a belt to tighten the waist to my size. My feet were bare and dirty from the damp forest floor.

We were leaning up against a tree trunk and Daniel was right beside Luke. He was banged up - dried blood and bruises on his face and neck. His clothes were torn and dirty. But his chest was rising and falling peacefully as he rested. I watched them both for a moment longer before remembering my own injury. The branch that was lodged in my chest was gone and my skin had healed into a raised pink scar already. I hissed when I pressed on the scar, it was still tender to the touch. I inhaled deeply and closed my eyes, stretching my body in all directions to try to familiarise myself with each part again. The moon was on the horizon, it would be morning soon.

I knew that I wouldn't be going back to sleep, so I decided to walk around instead. The sky was light enough that I could see the ground before me. It was quiet, the calm after the storm I suppose. Luke and Daniel must have moved us from where we encountered the bear, because the forest looked different. There was no remaining evidence of the fallen trees or the bear's corpse that I had ripped apart. The forest was beautiful, mosses and ferns growing from the ground. Huge trees, scaling high into the sky.

My head started spinning and my chest tightened. I remembered shifting and what I had done to protect Daniel. I gasped as I fell to my knees, a headache forming in my temples. I panted towards the ground, curling my fingers into the dirt and my vision blurred as tears formed in my eyes.

"It's okay, Melody." His calm voice came from behind me, and I lifted my head. "Just breathe."

Luke walked up behind me and held onto my shoulders, he took deep breaths, and I did the same. I wasn't sure why I was crying, but I couldn't stop myself. I fell back into his arms and allowed him to hold me. His arms felt so firm and warm. He held me tightly and kept his breathing steady. He let me cry in his arms for what felt like forever.

"I thought he was going to die." I finally said. I looked up towards Luke and he relaxed his arms enough but didn't let me go.

Luke gently brushed his thumb across my cheek, wiping away a tear. "He didn't though. Because of you, he didn't."

Luke cradled me in his arms, and cupped my face in his palm. I pushed my cheek into his touch and looked up at him. The sky had turned into the most beautiful violet as the sun began rising. Luke's deep brown eyes met mine, they were almost glowing. I could feel my cheek heat slightly as I noticed his pupils dilate.

His gaze did not waver.

His features were striking, his dark curly hair still a mess atop his head. He had large, bushy eyebrows that always seemed tense. He held his lips in a tight line, but something about how intensely he stared into my eyes gave him away.

His lips parted slightly and he leaned in an inch.

Daniel made a noise as he turned over where he was sitting against the tree and it broke our gaze. Both staring in the direction of the noise. Luke cleared his throat and stood up, offering me a hand to pull me to my feet. We walked back to Daniel quietly, my heart still trying to steady. We exchanged small glances towards each other on the quick walk back.

I changed into my own spare clothes but kept Luke's cargo pants on. They were much more practical than the cotton leggings I had packed for myself. Luke didn't seem to mind either.

"They look good on you." He said through a grin, as he brushed his hand through his curls. I turned away quickly to hide the smile on my face.

Daniel woke up shortly after and I checked him for any injuries before we started our journey again. He was almost untouched. I patched up a few small scrapes and he gave me a weary smile.

"Mel, that was crazy last night." Daniel said as he pulled his backpack on. "I know you told me you shifted, but seeing it was insane." He laughed and shook his head.

I laughed sarcastically, as I laced up the runners I had packed. Daniel didn't have any major injuries, although I noticed him hiding a limp when we set off. He would be too irritating if I pointed it out, so I made a mental note to keep an eye on it.

We walked for most of the day. The forest had a new lease of life after the storm last night. The rain had made the green leaves shine and stand tall. Rays of sunlight pierced through the treetops and dappled the forest floor.

Luke and I exchanged small glances and smiles as we walked, but neither said anything of what happened, or didn't happen earlier.

We came across a large fallen tree, too big to go around, we had to go over it. It was slightly caved in on one side. I didn't want to think about what giant monster had made the indent. Luke climbed up first and lent Daniel a hand up and over so effortlessly, you'd think Daniel weighed less than a feather. He reached his hand towards me and interlocked his arm in mine as he pulled me up. I sat on top straddling the branch as he was.

We were face to face and I felt his breath on my lips. Without a word, he slid off the branch and landed solidly on the ground. He turned and raised both his arms up and I slid off too. He caught my hips and slowed my descent and when my feet hit the ground, he kept his hands on my waist. We stared into each other's eyes for only a moment before turning to face Daniel, who was staring at us with a look of amusement.

"What?" I snapped.

"Nothing." He said, smirking and raising both his hands up in surrender. Luke seemed to smirk at that.

The day dragged on, and my muscles were aching more with every hour that passed. Luke noticed I was massaging my calf muscle when we had stopped to rest.

"How are you going?" He asked and sat down next to me.

"I am sore, my muscles." I replied.

"That happens to me too. Especially if it's been a while between shifts. And you did fight off a mutated bear." He patted my knee with his hand and stood up to walk away.

"Luke." I said to his back. He turned his body around to face me. "What happened last night?" I asked. He looked at me confused, so I added, "How did I shift knowingly?"

"Oh, that!" He let out a short laugh. "I don't know. Maybe my pendant was close enough to you?" He shrugged it off.

I nodded slowly, still not understanding. I remembered him being there too, in his other form. Speaking to me through his mind.

"Have you ever spoken to another creature like that before?" I asked.

"No. That was a first." He replied. "I didn't even know if it would work. But I remember back when Oscar and I were first shifting, in the lab. I could hear screaming, other people screaming, in my head. I was so drugged up, I thought I was hallucinating. But I recognised Oscar's voice one night, he was begging to die. For someone to end his suffering. I always wondered if that was just in my head, or if Oscar was really reaching out through his mind. So, last night, I thought that if I willed my mind to travel to you enough, that maybe you would hear me." He said in a low voice.

"Well, I heard you." I replied. My eyes locked with his and something deep within me stirred.

We continued walking and Luke told stories of when he was in the army. Before the war. We practiced the defence moves Luke taught us when we stopped for food. Not for fighting, but to help us have a better chance at escaping. Luke taught both of us some very simple, but effective moves that might work against an attacker. We stood opposite each other, and he walked us through the moves, one by one. I picked up the moves quickly, blocking Luke's blows and swinging myself out of the way. I knew he was taking it easy on me, but it felt good to get the moves right. It also felt nice to be so close to Luke. Daniel struggled to move as quickly as Luke. He lost focus easily and got frustrated quickly, it was easy for Luke would pin him to the ground.

"Again." Luke said as he bounced to his feet. Daniel was getting noticeably angrier each time Luke grounded him.

"See how he is getting mad, Melody?" Luke smirked at me from over his shoulder.

"This means that he isn't thinking. And not thinking, leads to..." He swivelled his leg behind Daniel, tipping him backwards.

Daniel fell flat on his back and groaned loudly.

Yelling profanities at Luke, Daniel stumbled to his feet again. He held a defensive stance and Luke turned away, walking towards me.

"That's enough for today, big guy." Luke said to Daniel. He held my gaze, but his attention was still on Daniel, who was now running towards Luke's turned back. Daniel flew through the air and wrapped his arms around Luke's shoulders. With little effort, Luke flipped Daniel over his shoulder and threw him to the ground. He kept a grip on his arms, so the impact was lessened.

"Before you hurt yourself." He smirked.

We practiced when we could, pairing off so we all had a chance to practice together. Watching Luke practice his combat moves, with Daniel or alone, was mesmerising. He moved so effortlessly, but with such intent and power behind him. Luke would fidget with his knife sometimes. I don't think he realised he was doing it though. Balancing it between his fingers and spinning it. He handled his weapons with such ease, especially the sword. Like it was an extension of his arm. I tried to imagine what he looked like on a battlefield, how lethal he would be. His raw strength and the smoothness of his movements would prove lethal. He would be terrifying to go up against.

"The more you practice the moves, the more natural they will feel. You won't be thinking as much when you're in an actual fight though. You will be in survival mode." Luke said, watching Daniel and I sparring.

We walked through the forest for days and I was thankful we didn't come across another mutated beast. And although we hadn't seen them yet, we knew the Snatchers were in the forest. Luke found snares and some traps they had set. A few camp sites with fires that had been put out. We were careful and kept quiet.

The days were repetitive; walk, rest, train, eat, walk, rest and so on.

At midday, we came to a man-made dam. The water was murky and smelt putrid, but Luke said there was a building on the far side which might be safe for us to rest in for the night. When we reached the far side, a small building came into view. It would have been for short term use, before the war. For workers to find shelter during the summer days. It was equipped with a toilet and a small room no bigger than an average bedroom. The bathroom was unusable, and the small room was covered in muck and grime from who knows what building up over the months. There was one window that had been shattered. Vines were now growing through it and into the room.

"Perfect." Luke said grinning, hands on his hips. Looking like he had just hit the jackpot.

"It's a roof over our heads." Daniel shrugged and went to clear some of the debris from the floor.

I looked around the room and decided to take a walk around the dam instead. It was so peaceful. The breeze was soft and took the edge off the fetid smell of the static dam water. I stood on the dam wall and took in the scenery. The dam hadn't been used in quite some time, and the railing was rusted and coarse under my palms. The mountains in the distance were hidden by low clouds, but the sun brightened the curves of the landscape. It would be setting soon, and we would face another night out here. Another day closer to reaching the safe haven.

I closed my eyes and took a deep breath. The wind rushed past me, smelling of the earth and the trees surrounding us. I inhaled the air deeply as the breeze flew through my hair taking with it small bits from around my face.

I couldn't help but think of our mother.

That she brought the Snatchers to our home and was going to give us over to them. A lump formed in my throat and my eyes burned. No matter how hard I tried to hate her for what she did. I wished she was here with us. The mother who would sing and dance while arranging flower bouquets, who would kiss a bruise or give us a sweet treat after dinner. The mother who took care of us and made us feel safe.

A tear ran down my cheek, and I opened my eyes, the wind stinging.

The version of my mother I wanted died a long time ago.

# Chapter 7

I took my time getting back to the building. Instead, I walked around the building and collected some firewood. The building wasn't that old, concrete walls, a tiny window and a tin roof. Nature had grown up the walls and over the roof. There was some graffiti on the walls too, unreadable tagging that had no doubt been done prior to the disaster. I grabbed small sticks and some dry leaves until my hands were full. Daniel and Luke had gone hunting and would be back soon, I hoped. My stomach rumbled at the thought of dinner.

When I got back to the small room, it was dusk and Daniel and Luke were still out, searching for food. They had cleared the floor enough that we would be able to sleep on it without catching some sort of disease. My mouth watered as I thought of all the foods I would eat at Illumina. Luke had mentioned they had fantastic food there. And they held a community dinner every week, where everyone brought a plate of food to share and caught up on the events of the week. It sounded so lovely.

A sense of normalcy that I craved.

I heard Daniel and Luke before I saw them. Laughing and carrying on as they got back to the room. Luke held two rabbits, both in great condition. Untouched by the radiation and well fed. We will be eating well tonight.

"Are you okay?" Luke asked as he came into the room.

I only nodded and he smiled back at me with that dazzling smile that lit up his face.

My cheeks burned.

Daniel prepared dinner and we all took our share. I had grown fond of the small rabbit meals we had eaten each night. The conversations that flowed between the three of us. I wondered for a moment, if none of this had of happened, if we would have ever met Luke. I shook the thought out of my mind and continued to enjoy Luke's story.

"So that's why we called him 'Shifty'." He said and Daniel burst into laughter. I hadn't heard the start of the story, but hearing the two of them laugh was enough to make me join in too.

A glimmer of hope shone around us.

~~~

In the morning, Luke and I woke up with the sun and decided to walk out on the dam wall.

"I think we should stay another night." I said into the wind.

"We can do that." Luke replied. "Illumina isn't that far now. Another day or two."
~~~

Luke stood right next to me, our shoulders almost touching. His hand brushed mine on the rusted railing of the dam wall. The sunrise was beautiful, it had a magical feeling about it. The orange gold sky reflected off Luke's skin in such a way that he looked as though he was made from gold. The wind brushed through his dark curls and they swayed gently across the top of his head. I stared at him. I couldn't look away.

He was beautiful.

"I am really glad I met you." I said.

"Yeah, you would've been toast if I hadn't come to save you." He jokingly nudged my side with his elbow.

"Do you want to try shift again?" he said and the smile was wiped from my face.

"Shift again? Like on command?" My heart pounded in my chest.

"Yeah, let's see if it really is my pendant. See if you can control it?"

I stared into the mountains, far off in the distance for a long while. I would have to, eventually, wouldn't I?

"Okay." I finally said. I knew Luke could feel me tense. He placed his hand on my shoulder and squeezed tightly.

We walked deep into the forest. Neither of us had said a word since telling Daniel where we were going and what we were going to do. He had opted to stay at the campsite and rest some more. Although he said he was fine, he still walked with a slight limp, favouring one side. Luke led the way, weaving through fallen trees and moss-covered rocks. The forest truly was magnificent. Rays of sunshine broke through the tall trees, casting beams of bright lights that reached the forest floor. Water droplets from condensation reflected the sun making the forest look as though it was covered in glitter.

"Okay, this looks like a good spot." Luke said as we came into a clearing.

We placed our bags and weapons down on the side and strode into the centre of the grassed area. And Luke started to undress.

"What are you doing?" I asked quickly.

"Well, I don't want to ruin my clothes." He laughed. "Don't worry, I won't look."

He turned his back towards me and I blushed as he removed his shirt. His toned back muscles tensing under the movement. He had healed scars crossing over his back slashing in different directions. I winced at the thought of what he had endured. He pulled off his pants and kept his underwear on. Piling his clothes with our bags.

We stood opposite each other, although he still faced away from me I could feel his attention on me. I slowly undressed too, leaving only my underwear on.

"Now what?" I said.

"What do you mean?" he laughed, back still towards me. "Now you shift."

"How?" I snapped.

"Well, how did you do it when the bear was attacking Daniel?"

"I don't know." I confessed. "It just happened. I was so worried that Daniel was going to get hurt, that's all I was thinking about."

"Right, well there isn't anyone in immediate danger here." He said, slowly turning to face me. His eyes upon me now, I felt exposed. He took me in with his eyes. My cheeks heated, but I held his gaze.

"How do you shift?" I asked with a bit more sass than intended.

His eyes met mine and he smiled. "I have a calmer approach. I like to breathe slowly, imagine myself in my strongest form and remember who I am. I don't let the creature control me."

He closed his eyes and started taking deep breaths in and out. I watched him as his body began to contort itself, his limbs snapping and changing. I wanted to turn away but his dark brown eyes stared straight into mine and I couldn't tear my gaze from him. I blinked myself out of the daze and he stood before me in his creature form. His huge, bulging muscles flexed under his weight as he readjusted his stance. Pushing himself to stand tall.

*Melody.* The words brushed my mind, and I took a step back.

"Luke." I almost whispered his name.

*It's your turn.* His voice sent a shiver up my spine and my whole body felt weak.

I closed my eyes and thought of myself in my creature form. Of the strength that I possessed when I was her. Deep breaths in and controlled breaths out. Nothing.

"It's not working." I said, staring at the grey creature in front of me.

His form stood tall, strong. I would've once been so terrified of him, but now I stood opposite him, staring at his beautiful dark eyes.

And he stared back.

*Clear your mind, Melody. You can do it.* His voice was deep, musky and so enchanting.

I did as he said. Closing my eyes again and willed my mind to clear. I took deep breaths again and listened to the surrounding forest. The sound of the wind passing through the trees and the blades of grass dancing in unison. The sound of far away birds who still had enough joy to sing and call to one another.

Deeper breaths, in and out. Feeling the earth under my feet and grounding myself, widening my stance.

I felt it then. My bones snapped, my skin boiled across my body.

I fell to my hands and knees. Clutching the grass so hard, trying not to lose myself.

*Breathe Melody.* His voice sliced through the agony splintering my mind. *I am here with you. It's Luke and I am here.*

I let out an animalistic scream as my body boiled over the edge.

*My eyes shot open and I saw him. The creature standing before me. I felt a deep growl slip out from my throat and I felt my lips curl over, exposing my teeth.*

"It's okay" The creature caressed my mind. I closed my eyes to savour his voice. "I am Luke." The creature said, placing a hand on his chest. "You are Melody."

I took a few steps forward, until we were only a breath apart. His dark brown eyes stared back at mine, and I felt his heart beating through the ground. I took in my surroundings and he did the same. I brought my hand up to touch his face and he leaned into my touch. My long spider-like fingers gently touched his cheek and moved down, across his neck and chest. His grey skin matched mine. His muscles tensed under my touch. He exhaled slowly as if he craved the touch more than I had. My wandering hand trailing his abdomen downward. His hand clasped around my wrist gently, stopping me at his navel.

I looked up and my eyes met his again. His grey lips parted into a smile.

"C'mon. Let's test these bodies out." And he took off into a sprint on all four legs.

I followed his command and ran beside him, our strides matched each other and we moved through the forest with such ease. I felt the forest floor under my feet, with each connection to the ground, I felt stronger and stronger.

I could get used to this.

# Chapter 8

I was absolutely exhausted after spending the day shifting with Luke. We shifted back and forth and ran through the forest all afternoon. I tried to send my voice to Luke but couldn't even manage a whisper. It was going to take a lot longer to master that one. Luke and Daniel went out to find dinner, and I stayed back to rest and get the fire going.

I had just started the fire when I heard footsteps outside.

"It's about time." I said jokingly.

When I stood and turned to face the doorway, I froze. The bits of firewood I had collected fell from my hands, thudding loudly around me.

In front of me stood a tall man. He was dressed in black, with a helmet covering his eyes and stopping above his mouth, which was curled into a sickening grin.

"We have been looking for you." The Snatcher sneered. Three more figures appeared behind him. Two men, smaller than the first but solid. The third stood back.

I was frozen with fear and Luke's training ran through my mind over and over. I couldn't fight off four people. I widened my stance and grounded my feet, trying to engage my muscles. The first man stepped through the door and the others followed in unison. He was much taller than me and had broad shoulders. I could try to use his size against him. As he lurched forward, I ducked down and slid through his legs, turning quickly to use both my feet to kick him right in his behind. He went stumbling forward and knocked his head into the wall. Two other Snatchers came forward, each grabbing an arm and hauling me up.

"Tough girl, huh?" The fourth Snatcher came forward and to my surprise, was a woman. She removed her helmet and revealed her face. She had a large scar running from the top of her head, over her eye and down her cheek. Half her head was shaved, and the rest was a short mess. The skin that I could see was covered in strange tattoo's, black ink traced along her body in swirls and shapes. She smiled from ear to ear, tucking her helmet under her arm as she circled me. The Snatchers on either arm gripped me tighter, steadying me so I had to face the woman.

"You've been a hard one to track down." She leaned in close. "Luckily we had your mothers help. She told us about your little *safe haven*." I whimpered as the new betrayal struck deep inside me.

I struggled to free my arms but the grip on the Snatchers was too tight, their fingertips digging into my arms. I watched the woman standing in front of me as she picked something from her teeth and examined it.

"You had us on a wild goose chase, girl." She said, "They will like you in the lab. Yes, you will be a good, strong subject." She let out a small laugh and waved her hand at the Snatchers holding me.

They dragged me out of the building and threw me to my knees. I slumped to all fours but raised my head enough to quickly search my surroundings for Daniel and Luke. I didn't want the Snatchers to capture them too. I couldn't see them with my quick glance, so I sat back on my knees and raised my chin. Staring the woman in the eyes. I bared my teeth at her to show the disgust on my face.

She came at me quickly and her hand wrapped around my throat. Squeezing tight. She pushed all her weight into her arms, and I lost my balance, falling back. She pressed hard and I couldn't breathe. I clawed at her, trying to reach her face to do any kind of damage. Gasping for air. My vision was blurring and black spots formed in the corner of my eyes. Slipping in and out of consciousness.

I opened my eyes to see a fist plummeting towards me and I blacked out.

I heard the muffled sounds of the Snatchers talking to one another, though I couldn't make out what they were saying. They dragged me by my feet, the gravel cutting into the back of my head. My arms dragged too, they felt numb. I tried desperately to open my eyes, but they were heavy, something clumped in my lashes stopping them from opening. I could smell the sweet tang of blood, fresh blood, as it swelled out of my nose.

The Snatchers stopped walking and let my feet drop to the floor with a thump. Pain ricocheted up my knees and they grabbed my arms again and hoisted me up and into a vehicle. I couldn't see anything, but I could hear the radio. Someone checked in with the location of where we were and the Snatchers responding promptly.

"We will be back before dark." A man's voice spoke.

I was laying down on a cold, hard surface. They strapped my wrists tightly so I couldn't move them even an inch.

"This might hurt a bit." The woman's voice was low and wet in my ear. Then I felt a sharp pain in my arm. I tried to retract it, but it was held in place. A warm sensation came across my body, my senses dulling and I felt like I might be sick. I tried again to move off the table, but my body gave out as my consciousness was slipping away. Just before the darkness overcame me, I thought I heard a voice, Luke's voice, clawing the back of mind.

*Melody!* He shouted. *Melody!*

# Chapter 9

My mind was drifting through a black abyss.

Peaceful and quiet.

I could feel my body, somewhere nearby, but I couldn't access it yet. I was floating aimlessly, waiting to return.

A lightning bolt of pain shot through my chest and I jolted. The room flashed into my vision and was gone just as quick. I waited for a moment longer and another shock of pain came crashing through me. I opened my eyes and the bright lights burned my vision, causing an immediate headache.

"She's back!" A voice exclaimed. "Stabilise her, now!"

I felt hands grabbing me from every direction. Jabbing, poking, pulling and holding me. I didn't try to move, because I couldn't remember how to use my body. I tried opening my eyes again and it was manageable, but the bright lights were still beaming down on me. As I squinted around the room, I saw four people wearing pristine white lab coats.

They were busying themselves, running from one side of the room to the other, writing things down on charts, or closely monitoring my vitals.

There was one man who stood at the back of the room. He wore a navy blue suit, his vibrant red hair was slicked back behind his ears. He didn't take his eyes off me.

I looked down at myself. My clothes had been removed and I was in a light blue hospital gown. My wrists and ankles were bound to the bed with thick leather straps. Each of my arms had a cannula running to separate machines. Unknown fluids were pumping into me from both sides.

Once the doctors and nurses were finished with their checks and jotting down their notes. One of them relayed their findings to the man in navy at the door.

"Good." He said in a deep voice. "Get out." They scurried off with their heads low before he had finished the command.

The man stalked over to the bed, eyes not wavering from mine. He stopped at the foot of the bed and crossed his arms over his chest. He cleared his throat as if he was going to speak but stayed silent. He was plump, his belt cutting into his waist. He had large dark circles under his eyes as if he was drained from his daily life. Stubble growing on his chin and his fingernails bitten down to the quick. He walked over to one of the fluid pumps and flicked the liquid running into my arm.

"So," he began. "My name is Dr Gelch." My heart quickened on the monitor as I remembered Luke's stories. His eyes flicked to the beeping, and he smiled as he realised my fear.

I stayed still, keeping my eyes on him. I couldn't move and felt the effects of whatever drug they had running through my veins.

"We need to wait until you're stronger before we can start running our tests." He stood at my side and rested his hand on top of the leather strap around my wrist. "But we're so glad you're here. You will be so helpful to our cause." He spoke monotone, as if he had recited those exact words thousands of times. He turned to walk out of the room but stopped at the threshold. "If you need anything, just call for the nurse." He pointed to a red button on the far wall. He smiled and left the room.

*Asshole!* I thought to myself.

I tugged and pulled at the leather straps, even though I knew it was hopeless. Defeated, I slumped back into the bed. My chest ached from the abrupt awakening and my thoughts tumbled through my head. Daniel and Luke. Did they know I had been taken? I remembered hearing Luke's voice in my mind and tried to send him a message. I had no idea how to do it or if it would work, but I had to try.

*Luke.* I pushed his name though my mind. *Luke, can you hear me?*

Nothing.

I tried to visualise him, standing in the forest, smiling at me. *Luke? Please.* I began sobbing.

I lost track of time - they always kept the lights on. My back was numb from the lack of movement. Nurses came into the room, took my vitals, pushed pills down my throat or injected medicine into my fluid lines and then left. No one spoke a word to me, nor I to them. When I felt awake enough to try to contact Luke, I did.

He never replied.

~~~

I didn't know how long had passed. Hours or days. One of the nurses had just finished changing over the fluid bag when a tall, lean man walked in holding a chart filled with messy bits of paper. His long lab coat glided in behind him as he opened the door wide.

He cleared his throat, and the nurse left the room.

"Hello, my name is Dr. Springer, and I will be overseeing you." He pushed his thick black glasses up his nose. His smile didn't quite reach his eyes. Eyes that were dull and tired. He had thin black hair and as much as he tried to hide it, I could tell he was balding. But he beamed with something, excitement maybe. "I will escort you to your first test now."

When I opened my mouth to speak, my throat caught. My tongue was so dry and my lips cracked. Instead, I nodded, no expression on my face. One of the nurses came back in and unplugged all the cords and lines running in and out of my arms. She smiled at me so sweetly and helped me to my feet.

Dr Springer led us down the corridor and the nurse held me tightly as I stumbled over my feet, trying to keep up. The corridor was narrow and all white. We passed door after door, each with a pin code lock on it and a binder of paper hung on the front. The binders had the patient's file and
~~~

information on them. Each one the same, only the picture and patient number differing. I could hear cries, screams or groans from behind some doors, when we passed them. Some of the doors were wide open and empty.

Dr Springer stopped at the end of the corridor and motioned to an elevator. The nurse ushered me in and then stepped back out. I held onto the handrail tightly, hoping my legs wouldn't give out.

"Thank you, Janice." Dr Springer walked in and stood closely beside me.

The nurse, Janice, gave him a shy smile and hurried off. He waved a passkey over the elevator lock and pressed a button labelled *BG*.

"I'm sure you're wondering what it is that you're doing here." He spoke.

I didn't move, just kept my face looking forward at the levels we passed as we went lower and lower.

"Well, it's simple. You're going to help us run some very straightforward tests." He used his hands a lot when he spoke, waving them around enthusiastically. "And we hope to gather enough data on all of these mutations." He spoke with such confidence, I almost believed him.

As the elevator slowed to a stop, the doors slid open and a large room was revealed. He placed his hand on my elbow and encouraged me to walk forward. I felt sturdier on my legs now, although I held my arms out to balance just in case.

We walked out into the room, it was huge. The ceiling was so far up I had to kink my neck to look. The walls were damp and covered in pipes, cords and machines. Some beeping intermittently, others had clouds of smoke wafting out. I looked around, taking it all in and I stopped in my tracks when I saw the cage in the middle of the room. There were desks and chairs stationed around the cage with more people in white coats sitting at them, writing on paper, filling in charts and monitoring screens.

"Magnificent, isn't it." Dr Springer said with a broad smile. I could tell that he was genuinely proud of the work they have been doing down here.

As we got closer to the cage in the centre of the room, inside it I saw a body lying on the ground. The cage was big enough for an elephant and the body looked so small inside it. Two men in white coats unlocked the cage door and rolled a stretcher trolley into the centre. They grabbed the woman's body and roughly flung her onto it. They wheeled her out and a few more people in coats went over to examine her body. They stuck needles into her arms and drew out some blood. Another took her temperature and checked other vitals.

When they were done, one of them yelled "Patient R2168 has expired! Order disposal." Just as casual as talking about the weather. They wheeled her off on the trolley and out into another elevator on the other side of the room.

"Your turn." Dr Springer smiled down at me. "Don't worry, patient R2168 has been extremely helpful in our studies. You will be too."

# Chapter 10

Dr Springer held my elbow tightly as he led me towards the cage, the other workers hosed out the concrete floor where the woman's lifeless body was laying just moments ago. The blood-tinged water rushed down the drain quickly, taking with it any remnants of the torture she endured.

I wished for a moment to melt into liquid and follow the flow of the water to freedom, to safety.

I thought of Luke again, that he had endured all of this too.

But he made it out.

I had to find the doctor Luke told me about, maybe he could help me escape, like he did with Luke. I looked around the room, taking it all in. Doctors and nurses running around. Did they all agree with what was going on here?

My arm was nudged again, and rage, or maybe it was fear, suddenly filled my body.

I ripped my arm from his grip and turned for the elevator. My legs felt uneven under the weight of my body as I pushed into a run. It felt like I was moving in slow motion, everyone's eye on me. None of them moved, not one person tried to catch me. When I slammed my body into the elevator door, I pressed the button repeatedly, only to be met with a low buzz and red flashing button. I turned my back to the door and slid down to a crouch. I gasped for air, panting from the small sprint I just made. The drugs still coursed through my veins, and I had been bedridden for too long, my strength had dwindled.

The room began to spin slightly and I lost my balance, falling forward onto my knees. I steadied myself on all fours and in the pit of my stomach, I felt it. The queasy feeling trying to push its way out.

*Oh no,* I thought to myself, *no, no, no, don't vomit.*

Just as the thought slipped through my mind I heaved, emptying the contents of my stomach. There wasn't any food, just acidic bile. My eyes watered and I heaved again. Dry reaching, over and over again until I was left with nothing.

My hands were shaking as I wiped my mouth. I felt so damn weak.

"Are you finished?" Dr Springer called from across the room, not even bothering to look in my direction.

I stood up, unsteady on my legs and held my chin high as I began the uncomfortable walk back to the doctors. Defeated and embarrassed.

My body was trembling and spent from the energy I had just wasted.

"I should have told you before, though, I didn't think it necessary," he paused long enough to look down at me, "You can't escape."

He handed a binder over to the man standing next to him, shoving him aside. And walked towards me.

"We need to get started. So, if you're done, follow me." He strode off towards the huge cage.

I reluctantly followed and three other workers were already in the cage waiting for me. They had set up a large, leather chair into the centre of the room. It had clearly been used many times, as the leather was falling to bits. My throat caught as I came to the centre of the cage, the damp air turning foul.

I cupped a hand over my mouth and tried to resist the urge to vomit again.

My eyes watered at the smell. Blood and other bodily fluids with the rusted iron bars of the cage, all mixed together to build a horrid and stale odour.

Dr Springer waved his hand at the chair and wordlessly motioned for me to sit. As I sat in the cold and slightly damp chair, the three other workers rushed to me and bound my wrists and ankles tightly in straps. Dr Springer was on the outer edge of the cage, preparing something large. I tried to see, but his body obstructed my view. My mind was racing with possibilities as to what they were going to do.

My thoughts went to Luke, what he had endured and that he got out. I took deep steady breaths to calm myself.

Luke got out. I could get out too.

I had to get out.

When Dr Springer turned, he held a helmet-like object in his hands. It was bigger than a bike helmet but held a similar shape. It had a few wires crossing over the top of it and a big tube running from one side of it, across the floor and into a machine on the outer side of the cage. Someone outside started the machine and it roared awake. Blowing smoke from the far side of it and vibrating through the concrete floor. It was so loud I could barely hear the words Dr Springer was barking at me.

"I am going to place this on your head." He yelled, veins popping out of his neck, "Hold still."

He roughly placed the helmet on my head and buckled it up. Tapping it once on top to make sure it was steady. He fiddled with the tube at the back for a moment and then gave me a thumbs up with a large grin spreading across his face.

One of the other workers came close to my face, holding something small and black.

He tried to shove it into my mouth, and when I resisted, he shouted, "Trust me, you're going to want this!"

My eyes adjusted to the shape in front of me, I realised it was a mouthguard. I opened my mouth and allowed him to put it in.

All the workers hurried out of the cage, following Dr Springer to the computers and monitors at least 15 feet away from the iron bars. Dr Springer was pointing to the screens and giving orders to the others. My eyes searched the room.

There were only two exits I could make out. The elevator I came down and the other elevator where they took the woman's corpse. No windows and almost a dozen people working. The room was dimly lit, and there were machines and objects on the floor I could hide behind but I had no idea how I was going to escape.

Dr Springer held up his hand, holding three fingers in the air and counted down.

Three . . . two . . . one . . .

My body jolted and seized. My arms trying to break free of the leather straps that now cut into my skin. Pain like I have never felt surged through my entire body. Pulsing like a heartbeat. I could feel every individual part of me, like I was on fire and in ice at the same time. My bones moved under my muscles and my muscles cramped and tensed. The veins under my skin begged to crawl out. My fingernails dug into the chair, bending them back and sending more pain through my fingertips. Someone was screaming in the distance, and I tried to pry my eyes open and to my surprise there was no one else.

It was me.

I was screaming.

My vision turned white and I felt my eyes roll into the back of my head. I tilted my head back, chin to the sky and screamed again, before everything went black.

# Chapter 11

When I opened my eyes again, I was back in the hospital room. Hooked up to the fluid pumps again and laying neatly in bed.

My head throbbed. I held my fingers to my temples and rubbed them, trying to dull the pulsing.

Questions rushed through my mind as I looked around the room - it looked the same as it did before I left. I needed to survive and I needed to escape.

My heart jumped as the door swung open and in came a nurse. The same nurse that had escorted me before.

What was her name?

*Think, think!* I thought to myself. "Janice?" I said cautiously.

She turned her head quickly towards me, startled that I spoke, let alone said her name. She would have been in her late fifties, maybe. She had greyish-silver hair that was swooped into a neat bun atop her head. She was shorter than me, though she still had an athletic build. "Yes?" She spoke softly.

"I-I don't know what I was going to say." I confessed. "I suppose I just wanted to speak to you, to somebody." I slumped into the bed, trying to make myself smaller.

"Oh." She smiled sympathetically at me and placed a tray of food, actual food on my bed. "Eat up but take it slow. You haven't eaten solids in the time you have been here."

I looked at the tray in front of me, my mouth was watering. It wasn't anything fancy, mash potato, broccoli, carrot and meat. It smelled wonderful. Janice smiled again at me and then left the room.

I scooped the food into my mouth in huge mounds. I was so hungry, I realised. When I had licked the tray clean, I sat my hand on my bulging stomach. I didn't care if I had made myself sick from overindulging. It was worth it. I couldn't remember when I had last eaten. Or how long I had been in here. I had no concept of time. The meal settled in my stomach and I leaned back onto the bed. Adjusting the pale sheet to cover my exposed legs. My head still throbbed. I wondered what happened in the cage. What was the purpose of that experiment?

The door opened and I was eager to speak to Janice again, maybe make an ally here. Maybe I could ask her questions about the tests.

When the figure walked into view, my heart stilled. Dr Gelch came through the doorway, closing the door behind him and stopped at the foot of my bed.

"I heard you went to the cage today." His voice made my skin shiver. I nodded slowly. "I also heard you tried to run." He walked to my side, and I stiffened at his closeness. He leaned over, his breath hot in my ear.

"Let me make myself perfectly clear." His hand was quick as lightning, wrapped around my neck. I choked and grabbed at his thick fingers as they squeezed. I could draw in breath, but it made my eyes water, his grip kept firm on my throat. Meant as a threat, not to kill me.

"You cannot run. You cannot escape. You will never leave. And once I am done with you, I will discard you, like I have the rest." His voice came out raspy and harsh. A violent side of him showing.

I blinked quickly and I turned my eyes to stare directly at him. He held my throat for a moment longer and I thought I might pass out before the door swung open and Janice walked in. Dr Gelch let me go and straightened his shirt. I drew in a gasping breath and held my throat coughing. Her eyes darted between me and the doctor, but she didn't speak a word.

"Do I make myself clear?" He spoke with a steady and calm voice now.

I nodded in response, and held onto my burning throat, tender with forming bruises where his fingers were.

Dr Gelch walked out, passing Janice, who held her gaze to the floor. Once he was gone, she came to the side of the bed and picked up the empty tray. She started to walk away, before stopping at the foot of the bed, back still turned to me and placed a gentle hand on my foot, patting it once and then she left.

I slouched into the bed, hoping it would swallow me up and I could disappear forever.

Dr Gelch's words had stung, *you will never leave*, but he was wrong because I was going to escape.

Even if I died trying.

~~~

The next few days went by quickly and slowly at the same time. Every minute dragged on but before long, my next meal arrived and I knew I was closer to the next day.

I was awarded decent food when I complied with the tests and I was given butter and bread when I did not cooperate. I hadn't gone to the cage again. But Dr Springer had promised I would soon. He said that I needed to rest between the harder tests, or I would 'burn out'.

Janice didn't come back to my room and I wondered if she was purposely avoiding me. The other nurses didn't reply to me if I tried to talk to them, they just nodded or completely ignored me. Most of them were young, younger than me and looked at me like I was a disgusting beast.

One being particularly cruel to me.

Any spare moment I could find, any extra energy I mustered up, I would try to contact Luke.

He never answered though.

I spent my days in the small room. Mercifully I wasn't strapped to the bed anymore, but it didn't matter because they had me so drugged up that I couldn't even think of standing without assistance. I tried to remember the things
~~~

that Luke had told me about his time in the Lab. About how he escaped. But my mind felt like there was a fog covering those memories.

Thankfully Dr Gelch hadn't paid me a visit again, though I did flinch every time the door opened. Hoping it wasn't him. The nurses were quick with their rounds, in and out without any lingering.

They changed the sheets to my bed every now and then. Making me stand in the corner of the room facing the wall while they did. I had to hold onto the wall to stop myself from collapsing. It was the only time they left the door open while I wasn't in the bed. The laundry trolley didn't fit in the room, so they would have to move between the bed and the door to change the sheets. That might be the only chance I get to escape. I would have to time it right though. Try to build up my strength again and figure out a way to stop them from drugging me.

I stood in the corner of the room while the nurse changed the sheets, swaying slightly as my knees trembled. After the nurse finished, she ushered me back to bed and placed a cup of water on the table next to me.

"You must drink this, all of it." She said quickly. "Dr Springer is coming to see you soon." And she left without waiting for my reply.

I did as I was told and the cool water rushed down my throat with ease. I felt my body warm. I didn't even realise I had an aching headache until it vanished all at once. And my eyes became clearer, the fog surrounding my head lifted.

I looked at the empty cup in my hands. It must have been laced with something.

"*Luke!*" I pushed through my mind. "*Luke, are you there?*"

Silence. Utter silence. So I tried again.

"*Luke, please.*" I almost began sobbing.

"*Melody! You're alive!*" His voice caressed the back of my mind and tears rolled down my cheeks.

"*Luke, I don't have much time. I am alive. I am in the Lab. Dr Springer is coming soon.*"

There was no response for some time and I began to think I had imagined everything.

"*Luke?*" I tried again.

"*I am coming for you.*" Was all he said before Dr Springer came through the door.

# Chapter 12

"Good afternoon." Dr Springer said with a wicked grin, flicking through the paperwork in front of him. "You have been doing so well with our tests. I am very impressed. We get to go back to the cage today." He sounded excited, like it was a reward for me.

I gave him no response and kept my face blank. Janice appeared in the doorway, a weak smile on her lips as our eyes met.

"Unhook all the leads and get her ready to move." Dr Springer ordered the nurse and she quickly moved to my side. Dr Springer left the room for a moment and I decided to try my luck.

"What was in the drink?" I asked, no more than a whisper. Janice didn't answer, as if she were worried Dr Springer might hear her. "I haven't seen you for a while." I said to her instead.

"Oh yes dear, I have other duties." She smiled as she gently detached the IV drip in my arm.

"I wondered when I'd see you again." I spoke softly.

"I am usually only here to escort you to the elevator, and when you arrive back to your room. The other nurses take care of the rest." She put her hand on my forearm and gently patted my arm.

"How long have you been here?" I asked. I needed as much information as I could get.

"A while, dear." She looked into my eyes and I could've sworn I saw grief flash across her face.

"Janice!" Dr Springer called from the hallway. The nurse began to fumble and quicken her job. I realised then, that she feared him.

I grabbed her hand before she moved away and she turned to look at me. "You have to help me." I whispered. "Please."

Her eyes became glassy as she held back her tears. She opened her mouth to speak but Dr Springer walked in and she turned to finish her job without another word. Once I was unattached from the pumps, machines and leads, Janice helped me to my feet. I clung to her arm as she led me out of the room and into the bright hallway. Dr Springer walked in front of us, he was too close for me to speak to Janice.

So instead, I squeezed her arm twice, firmly but not hard.

She looked up at me, her eyes still glassy with tears she held back. Her other features were unreadable. We stopped in front of the elevator door and she let go of my arm. I braced myself on the railing inside the elevator and stared at the nurse, but she did not look at me.

Not once.

"Thank you, Janice." Dr Springer said. And the doors began closing.

I didn't dare take my eyes off hers as she vanished behind the doors. But she kept her eyes low, my heart sank.

The elevator passed each level quickly and the doors opened sooner than I had hoped. Dr Springer led me out into the huge room as he did all those days ago. Hand gripped firmly on my elbow. I wasn't sure if it was to stop me from running or to help me keep stable as I walked. The room looked the same as it had the first time I saw it. The room was dark and gloomy. Only lit by the yellow-orange-tinged lights hanging on the outer walls. The room smelt stale, and damp. Just like the first time I was brought to this room. There were no windows or any airflow down here. In the centre of the room stood the cage. My shoulders tightened and the hair on my body stood on its end as we neared the horrid chamber.

"So, today is simple." Dr Springer's voice came out of nowhere. "Same as last time, but a little amped up." He stopped me next to the monitoring screens, and I gazed down to look at what was on it.

An image of a human body appeared on the fuzzy screen, rotating in a full circle. Showing every angle of the body. And on the screen next to it, was an image of a creature. I looked between the two images as they rotated in sync. They must monitor my human form and my creature form when I shift.

Dr Springer moved between me and the screens, blocking my view. My eyes met his. He wore that same wicked smile he always did, showing off his untamed and yellow stained teeth. "Ready?" He said with excitement.

I gave one nod in reply, even though I was certainly not ready.

The only way I was going to get out, would be to get through these tests. Until I could see Janice again. I had a feeling that she could be my way out.

"Excellent." He led me into the cage. The leather chair taunting me with every step I neared.

The cage had been freshly hosed out. No doubt cleaning the excrement and any trace of the previously tortured victim. I sat down and gripped the arms of the chair hard. Two men in lab coats came to my sides and strapped me into the chair. Tight enough that my wrists ached immediately. The helmet was roughly placed on my head and the mouthguard shoved in. It tasted like foul plastic. I held my stare at Dr Springer and he held mine. I was going to escape. But first, I was going to kill him.

He held his hand above his head and grinned his wicked grin towards me. As if he could read my thoughts and dared me.

I let my mind and body go numb, preparing for what was to come. Even with the rising fear inside me, I took deep, steadying breaths.

Three... Two... One...

~~~

I was wet, drenched.

My eyes opened quickly as I gasped and thrashed around. Pain shot through my entire body like a lightning bolt. I was lying on the cold concrete floor of the cage. A hose drenching me in water. Blood swirled around me and down the drain. I tried to get up but was too weak. I lay back in the filth surrounding me.

The workers rushed around quickly, unhooking all of the leads they had put on my body. Some began to clear the chamber, carrying destroyed objects out of the cage. I struggled to steady my vision as I lay on the floor. There was so much blood, I realised. I tried to look over my body, checking for any wounds. I was naked. No wounds, cuts or bruises.

*Whose blood is this?* I thought to myself.

"Get her up and take her back to her room now." I recognised Dr Springer's raspy voice. Two male nurses grabbed me by my arms and threw me up onto a trolley. I tried to move my arms but they were limp, it felt like my brain had been disconnected from my entire body. The heaviness of my arms and legs made it seem impossible to move them at all.

"W-what... h-happened?" I whispered through laboured breaths.

No one answered. Maybe no one heard me.

Instead, they tied me to the trolley and placed a white sheet over me, instantly wet with the water still covering my body. I slipped in and out of consciousness during the elevator ride back and through the hallway that led to my room. The two nurses stuck closely to each side of the trolley as
~~~

they wheeled me down the bright hallway. The fluorescent lights flashed on the ceiling, as we passed each of them. I was transferred from the trolley and onto the bed, where Janice was waiting with a fresh hospital gown.

"Thank you gentlemen." She said sweetly. "I'll take it from here." and with that, they left, closing the door behind them.

Janice gently washed off any remnants of the blood and torture I had just endured and dressed me in a new gown. I was still slipping through my consciousness but knew I had to try to ask for help again.

I tried to lift my arm and it felt like gravity pulled against me, but I managed to land my hand across her arm. She stopped what she was doing and looked at me.

"J-Jan-ice." I managed with a raspy voice. "P-Please... help me." I tried to hold her gaze, but I slipped out of my mind again and saw nothing but darkness.

I could hear the nurses moving about in my room. Fiddling with the cannula in my arm and tending to the beeping machines every now and then. But I couldn't see them. I just drifted through a black abyss. With no destination. I felt weightless. I wasn't flying. I wasn't falling. I just simply was. I felt peaceful and scared at the same time. My body wasn't here, but my mind was. I'd find my way back soon, but for now, I wanted to rest.

I was jolted into reality abruptly and when I opened my eyes, Dr Gelch stared back at me. I instinctively tried to move away from where he stood, but I was tethered to the bed yet again. Ankles and wrists bound tightly to all the corners.

My body had begun healing at an even quicker rate. As if the tests and medication had strengthened the creature inside me. Any injuries I sustained during the tests would heal completely by the next morning. Leaving only a small, pink scar in their wake.

If I didn't heal so well, I knew I would've had wounds from the tight leather straps that bound me to the bed.

My heart rate on the monitor quickened as the fear in my chest rose.

"No need to get upset." He stood at the foot of my bed and casually waved a hand in my direction. In his usual navy suit that was at least one size too small for his round stomach. His vibrant red hair brushed backwards, behind his ears and his chin stubble that looked coarse and scratchy.

"I just wanted to go through some of your results for the test you completed two days ago."

*Two days ago?* I thought to myself. *Have I been unconscious for two days?*

"You did exceptionally well. We will be keeping you on for the next round." He held a touchscreen tablet in his hand and took a few steps closer to me, my body tensed in response. "Do you want to see how well you did?" He grinned and I knew he wasn't actually waiting for my reply.

He held the screen in front of me and a video was waiting to play. Dr Gelch clicked the play button and my eyes were fixed on the screen. It took me a second to realise what I was watching, but I recognised the cage. It was footage from that room, all those levels below us.

As though he could read my expression, he said, "Ah yes. I like to watch from afar. It can get pretty messy down there." He chuckled to himself. His stomach jiggled through his shirt. "Not really into the whole blood and gore stuff myself."

I didn't take my eyes off the screen.

There was a young blonde woman sitting on the leather chair in the middle of the cage. It was hard to see what was going on because the footage was fuzzy and taken from far away. They must have a camera set up on one of the walls. To record their torture down there for their own sick pleasure.

The woman sat there for what felt like ages, the workers scurrying around. Then I noticed Dr Springer standing near the monitors, hand in the air. After his countdown there was a zap of light from inside the cage. There was no sound to the video, but I swore I could hear phantom screaming in my head.

I blinked quickly and leaned into the screen in front of me.

It was footage of me. I was the woman.

A lump formed in my throat as I watched the video in shock. The woman's body, my body, contorted in all sorts of ways, her body breaking free of the straps holding her and she fell to the floor. In only a moment, the woman mutated into a creature. The helmet sat tightly at the top of the creature's head and the dark figure crashed around inside the cage. The workers in lab coats neared the cage and took down notes. The creature inside was absolutely feral. Smashing its huge body into the bars and trying to slice the air apart. The workers around the cage pressed buttons and the creature reacted physically. They were torturing it, somehow, through the helmet it wore. It held its head and cried out in pain as the workers looked on, laughing and writing down their results. Dr Springer made some very small movements on the monitor screen in front of him and the creature stilled. Just stood there, as though it was in a trance. A chill ran down my spine. Then from the far corner of the screen, a nurse wheeled a trolley into the frame. Lying on the trolley was a human body, wearing only a small cloth for privacy. They stopped just before the cage doors. With a wave of Dr Springer's hand, the cage doors were opened. The nurse stood for only a moment, wary of the monster inside the cage, then wheeled the body into the centre. The creature just stood there, not acknowledging the nurse or body at all. The body was pushed off the trolley and left lying on the floor. The nurse injected the body with something and then hurried out of the cage, taking the trolley with them. The body moved, awakening slowly. The creature was still and unmoving. My eyes watered as I realised what was about to happen, what I was about to do.

The body, the man, stood up and although I couldn't hear him, I knew he was screaming.

Pleading with the nurses and doctors. His arms outstretched through the bars of the cage, as far away from the creature as he could get. Dr Springer began pressing buttons on his screen again and the creature, still in a trance, turned to the man, and ripped him apart.

Dr Gelch took the screen away. "Impressive, isn't it?" he said, chuckling to himself again.

Silent tears rolled down my cheeks and dripped onto my hospital gown. I could hear my heartbeat thumping in my ears. I said nothing as my eyes met Dr Gelch's, his sickening grin filled his face. The circles under his eyes grew darker every time I saw him. I cried without any emotion showing on my face, staring into his soul.

"Thank you for proving to be of such use." Was all he said before quietly leaving the room and closing the door hard behind him.

I stared after him, tears still streaming down my face. I made a silent promise that I would kill him too.

# Chapter 13

The tests continued every few days, getting increasingly more intense.

Although, I never remembered much.

Janice would help wash and dress me afterwards, but we scarcely spoke. I wasn't strapped to the bed anymore, which was a little mercy. And the nurses escorted me to relieve myself twice a day, morning and night. The walk to the bathroom was short. Across the hall and two doors down. I was strapped to a bar on the wall and a nurse stayed in the room with me. But I was glad to leave the room.

Dr Gelch paid me a visit to show me new footage and I watched in disgust as I tore apart another person, limb from limb. I was totally under their control, in some sort of trance.

The helmets were some sort of mind control device that Dr Springer controlled. They were creating deadly weapons.

"Good morning." Dr Springer said as he entered my room. I became accustomed to having doctors and nurses enter and exit, that it didn't faze me anymore. I was so numb, I wasn't sure if it were the drugs keeping a haze over my mind, or if I was genuinely giving up.

"Today is a new and exciting test." He looked as excited as he sounded, almost jumping for joy. "Dr Gelch has been very impressed by you, so he has asked me to accelerate your tests."

I had the other nurse to escort me today, not Janice. Which was a shame. This nurse, whose name I hadn't learned, was horrible. She looked at me with disgust, as if I were carrying some sort of disease that she could catch if she were to show me an ounce of humanity, and she was rough.

"Get up." She barked at me after unhooking my lines. She grabbed my arm tightly and pushed me forward.

"No special drink today?" I asked with a little sass.

Every time I went to the cage, they gave me a cup of water laced with some sort of stimulant. Which lifted the fog and I felt aware, almost normal. And best of all, I could try to contact Luke. Sometimes it worked and sometimes it didn't. I was only able to get out short sentences, but it was enough. I knew Luke and Daniel were coming for me and to be ready when they did.

"No." Was all she replied and pushed me harder through the doorway.

She could be beautiful, if her face wasn't held in a constant scowl. She was young, in her early twenties. With long black hair, tightly woven into a plait and brought over her shoulder to the front. She had smooth pale skin, rosy cheeks and eyes as dark as a starless night. But the scowl she wore twisted her face in a way that made her look permanently furious.

We followed Dr Springer down the hallway, just like we did every other time. I was slightly unsteady on my feet but didn't dare hold onto the nurse walking beside me, in case she bit my hand off. When we came to the end and usually turned for the elevator, we turned the opposite way, through a different door. Another long depressing hallway awaited, this one had no doors or windows.

Just a long empty hallway.

It didn't take long to reach the end and when Dr Springer opened the door with his passkey, he stood to the side, allowing the nurse to push me through first. It looked like a bathroom. Porcelain white tiles lined the floor, with the darkest grout, making them stand out. They shined as if they were brand new. The walls were also tiled, but with larger tiles that were light grey in colour. In the centre was a bathtub, filled with water.

I wasn't expecting this to be a relaxing bubble bath, not when I saw the huge machine standing at the base of the bathtub. A few cords ran from the back of the tub, across the floor and to the monitor on the wall. There were two large tubes running into either side of the tub and coiled through the inside of it. And of course, a helmet. I kept my face expressionless as Dr Springer explained what the next two hours would entail.

I was to be submerged in the tub, the helmet tightly fitted. And an electrical shock was going to be sent through the water. They would keep turning up the electric current until I was in the *in-between state*, he called it. The state of my mind where I was about to shift, but they would turn the current back down, so I didn't shift. And this would repeat until I was unable to continue. They wanted to monitor my brain throughout this process, for their data and experiments.

"We need to make sure the electric shock doesn't go above here." Dr Springer pressed his finger on the dial, well into the red section. Showing the nurse. "We don't want to kill her." He warned the scowling nurse, and she nodded.

I wondered if Janice asked not to be on this rotation, because this was just torture. She seemed too sweet and innocent to be here.

Dr Springer turned to me, "When a sufficient amount of electrical current passes through the body, it can disrupt normal physiological functions." He took a step closer to me and my body tensed.
"Including your heart. And we don't want that to stop. Not today anyway." He laughed and walked over to the wall. He tapped at the monitor mounted there. "Dr Gelch has instructed us to keep you alive."

The nurse nudged me towards the bathtub. "Get in." I started to remove my gown. "No need to undress." She said pointing over to the fresh gown and towel sitting on a small table in the corner of the room.

I tested the water with my toe first and to my surprise, it was warm. Goosebumps covered my skin and a shiver raced up my spine as I climbed in. The water felt so nice on my skin. It was unfortunate that the first bath I have had in god knows how long, was going to torture me. I slipped deep into the bath so that the water covered my body. Although the water felt heavy on my chest, my body felt weightless. The nurse placed the helmet on my head. I knew she was being purposefully rougher than needed, but I knew to keep my mouth shut.

Dr Springer finished what he was doing on the monitor and came to the edge of the bath.

"We will be watching the whole time. No need to worry." He tapped my shoulder, in an almost compassionate way. I tried to resist raising my eyebrow at him. "Two hours and you're done. Hook her up Sophia." He said, walking out of the room.

Sophia, the nurse, grabbed a mask attached to a tube. It looked like something out of a nightmare.

"This is so you can breathe." She spat out at me.

Then grabbed my chin and forced my head upwards. She pushed a mouthguard between my teeth and shoved the mask over my face, covering my mouth and nose. It was shaped like a triangle, with the tube exiting dead centre. Then tightened a strap that circled around the back of my head.

It felt suffocating.

I tried to steady my breaths and get used to breathing through the machine. I felt my eyes tear up as fear filled my body. Sophia smirked at me and shoved my head under the water without warning. She held me under for a moment before letting go. I didn't resist her. There was no point. The water bubbled and swirled around above me, making it almost impossible to see. I tried to surface but couldn't. The back of the helmet had been hooked to the base of the tub. I tried harder to pull my head out of the water to no avail. My wrist was grabbed then and tethered to the side of the bath. Of course they had to strap me down, again. The other wrist was grabbed too and tied firmly in place.

I could just make out the distorted figure of the nurse leaning over the tub. She smiled a wicked grin through the rippling water and then waved at me from above the tub, disappearing after the doctor.

I took breaths as deeply and as calmly as I could. The mask made it hard to fully fill my lungs. I closed my eyes under the water and tried to imagine I was somewhere else. I heard three quick taps. They sounded like someone tapping on metal. Then I felt the vibrations surrounding the tub. The machine at the base had kicked into gear and was rumbling to a start. My body pulsed under the warm water, my heart pounding loudly. Then the first electric shock rushed through my body. Starting with my head, the shock travelled quickly down my spine and through my arms and legs.

Unbearable pain shot out of my fingertips as they gripped the rim of the tub. Every muscle in my body tensed, cramping and spasming with each pulse of the shock. I clamped down hard on the mouthguard and kept trying to breathe. Three quick taps on metal again and the shock increased. My body was shaking and I felt myself losing consciousness. As much as I tried, I couldn't control my breathing.

*In and out.* I thought to myself. *Breathe Melody. You need to breathe.*

My breaths steadied and my body felt numb. I could still feel myself trembling, but my mind became detached. Three more taps and the machine increased the electrical current again. Still numb, my body began thrashing and I could feel the water from the bath was being thrown around the room. Splashing over the tiles surrounding me. I opened my eyes and watched the dim room around me. My vision distorted from the ripples and splashing of the water.

I took deep and intentional breaths. Trying to calm myself for what was coming.

I could feel my mind slipping away, I couldn't hold on for much longer. Three more taps and the pulses increased again. My body thrashed uncontrollably and I could see my white knuckles gripping on to the side of the tub, drenched in the water that was being thrown over the sides.

I was almost ready to let the tub consume me, when Luke's voice floated through my mind.

*Hold on Melody. Just hold on.* His voice sang to me. I wasn't sure if I had dreamed it.

I closed my eyes tightly and took a few more deep breaths. I felt a wave of calmness flow over me and the thrashing stopped. I pictured Luke and Daniel, sitting around one of our campfires. They were laughing and sharing a rabbit for dinner.

Luke's face illuminated by the flames. Orange and red embers floating around the air surrounding them.

I tried to send a message to Luke's mind, but I could feel the message bounce back as if it ricocheted off an invisible wall in my mind. I took a few more deep breaths and I tried again.

*Luke...* I pushed through my mind. Trying not to scream. *"Luke!"*

# Chapter 14

*Luke*

*"LUKE!"*

I shot up, pain tearing through my head.

A scream escaped me and I grabbed my head with both hands, worried it might explode. Pain shot through me again, coming in waves, pulsing. I tried to look around the dismal campfire that Daniel and I had made the night before. The fire was no more than embers now. My eyes squinted in the dark night, pain still coursing through my mind. It pulsed, like an electric heartbeat.

"Daniel!" I managed to get out.

He awoke and quickly came to my side, "Luke, what's happening?" He stared at me through terror filled eyes.

"It's Melody" I said through my raspy voice. "Something is wrong!"

I held on to my head tightly as the pain surged again and again. Crouched over my knees, I placed my head on the ground and squeezed my eyes shut. I tried to take deep breaths, but I felt winded. Still crouched over, my head drummed into the ground.

It felt like hours has passed by and then it all stopped.

I blinked my eyes a couple times, trying to focus my vision and slowly released my head.

"Luke?" Daniel asked, cautiously sitting next to me. "What happened?"

"I heard her. She screamed my name." I said with more terror than intended. "And then all I could feel was pain." I stared up at the stars.

~~~

The sting of her voice still lingered on my mind when I woke in the morning. I had dozed in and out of sleep for the hours until sunrise. The sheer terror of how Melody sounded haunted me when I closed my eyes. Daniel didn't ask too many questions about what happened last night. We both knew that Melody had sent some sort of message to me. What I didn't tell Daniel, was my assumption that Melody was feeling that pain when she sent the message. A cry for help.

I shuddered at the memory of the torture I endured at the lab. The torture that Melody was now experiencing.

We had to get her back.

Melody had been captured over two weeks ago. I would wake most nights with nightmares. Seeing my own memo-
~~~

ries from my time in the lab, only they were warped, with Melody in my place instead.

The day she got captured, Daniel and I were walking back to the building we were camped at for the night, when we heard her scream. We raced back, but by the time we got there, the truck was speeding away. There was blood on the stones where Melody had been dragged to the vehicle. We ran after the truck, but we weren't quick enough. I tried to shift, but Daniel stopped me. After arguing like stubborn fools, we decided we would have a better chance of getting her back together. We tracked the Snatchers back to the city edge, where we lost them. I had to dig deep to remember the way to the lab. I had been so drugged up when I escaped, that I almost had no recollection of those first few hours. Oscar was with me back then, when he and I made it out together.

Daniel and I were hopeless though, until Daniel took charge. He said he had heard some things on the streets about the whereabouts of the lab. So together, we found our way. We came to an underground tunnel entrance, it would have looked like any normal abandoned tunnel, if it weren't for the four fully armed hulking brutes stationed along the entrance.

"Now what?" I said to Daniel as we crouched behind the neighbouring building. "There is no way we can just walk straight in, they will call for back up and we will be toast before we have even tried."

Daniel had been quiet the whole journey back to the city, I put it down to him being upset about the Snatchers taking his sister. But this felt different. Like he was hiding something.

"Hello? Daniel?" I shook his shoulder gently.

"I have an idea." Daniel finally said. "But you have to trust me." I nodded and listened to his plan.

~~~

After Daniel told me everything, it was hard not to judge. But I had promised him that I would turn a blind eye until we got Melody out. Then we would deep dive into everything. For now, Melody was the top priority. We could use his extensive knowledge of the lab to our advantage.

"I just need fifteen minutes. Then I will signal for you." Daniel nodded. His idea seemed far-fetched, but it was the only one we had right now. Other than for me to shift and break down the facility. Daniel wasn't a fan of that idea, he thought we would both just end up dead.

"What's the signal?" I asked, eyes on the four soldiers.

"You'll know." He smirked and walked away.

He was going to approach them from a different street. Said that was the way he'd usually come and that they were less likely to suspect something. Unlikely though. I knew men like that in the army, all muscle and no brains. They probably didn't even remember his name. I sat quietly waiting, not patiently, because I wanted to charge in there and rip everyone to shreds. But I promised Daniel we would try his way first. He finally came into view and I held my breath as one of the soldiers noticed him strolling towards them.
~~~

"Ah! Dan." The tall man covered in muscles said cheerily. "It's been a while, hasn't it?" He nudged the soldier standing next to him, who turned to see.

Okay, so they did know his name then. The others turned to watch him as he neared. All of them wore a friendly smile on their face.

"Heard your family got into a bit of trouble, mate?" The third one laughed as Daniel stopped in front of them. Daniel started talking to them quietly, too quiet for me to hear. They must have been very friendly then. My thoughts tumbled through my mind. Daniel wasn't lying when he said he knew them. He had been working for them since his father was killed. Helping them create weapons and instruments to use for their experiments. I realised that my thoughts had gotten the better of me and I was now filled with rage. When I looked towards the entrance again, two of the soldiers and Daniel were gone.

They'd taken him in.

"C'mon Daniel." I whispered. Suddenly very aware of how risky this plan was. Daniel was knowingly helping the doctors in the lab, to create torture devices for the creatures. Was he on their side? If he really was buddied up with them, he could easily go to Dr Gelch and tell him our plan, to help Melody escape. He could get me captured too. I began to panic a little as I realised, I had just given myself up, worse, I may have just killed Melody. My heart raced, my eyes searched the entrance for any bit of movement. Then one of the soldiers dropped to the ground. So silently,

I would've missed it had I not been watching so intensely. Then, in a matter of seconds, the other man dropped too.

Daniel appeared at the entrance alone, waving his hand high in the air. I raced over to him.

"I thought you were going to stab me in the back for a second there." I said, nudging him playfully. A nervous laugh escaping my lips.

"Regardless of my past. They have my sister, Luke. I am going to make the bastards pay." His voice was low.

A smile appeared on my face, I was relieved. "So how long do we have before they wake up?" I asked.

"They won't." Daniel turned and strode off into the darkness of the tunnel.

# Chapter 15



*Melody*

Firm hands grabbed my arms and tore me from the bath. I fell to the floor and lay splayed out. My saturated gown clung to my body as I tremored and jolted with each phantom electric shock. I took shallow breaths, all too aware of the mask that was still suctioned to my mouth and nose. When I opened my eyes, Sophia was standing over me, her arms drenched up to the elbows from dragging me out of the tub. She looked frantic, panting and her eyes wide with anger.

"You're not supposed to die." She spat through gritted teeth.

She ripped the mask from my face and I coughed and spluttered as I tried to fill my lungs with air. I tried to speak, but I wasn't sure I remembered how to. My mind felt foggy again, like I wasn't back in my body yet. Sophia began th task of un-attaching me from the machines, but she left me laying on the wet floor. I was cold, the temperature of the water had cooled drastically, and I was laying in my soaking wet hospital gown.

"She's fine." Sophia spoke into a microphone attached to the wall. "Got her out just in time, I think."

She sat down on a stool and began writing things down on her paperwork. Only eyeing me every so often, to check that I was still breathing.

I didn't try to move or get up, I just lay on the floor, staring at the ceiling. It was covered in small tiles, creating some sort of an image. I hadn't noticed it before. It was a mosaic of the sun. Different yellows and oranges all placed together to make a rather beautiful scene.

Sophia sat in the corner for what felt like a lifetime, and then cleaned up the cords from the machine. Once she was done, she crouched next to me.

"I need you to get up and get dressed." She nudged my shoulder and to my surprise, helped me to my feet.

She was less pleasant when she made me dry and change my gown by myself. Still unsteady from the electrical bath I'd just taken, it took much longer than either of us had the patience for. Once I was dressed, she knocked twice loudly on the door. It swung open in response and another nurse stood in the hallway with a wheelchair. I was very grateful to see the wheelchair, since walking the small distance from the bathtub to the door had already resulted in my legs giving out once. The nurse with the wheelchair smiled sweetly and helped me to sit down.

"Take her back to her room." Sophia said, monotone. "And get her something to eat."

The nurse nodded and wheeled me away quickly. Sophia walked into a room I hadn't noticed before, next to the one we had just left. I gazed in as we strode past the doorway. Dr Springer was sitting on a chair with a monitor in front of him. It was flashing with red warnings across the screen.

"I don't know what happened." He spoke softly but irritated. "I know, sir. But we didn't..." I couldn't hear the rest as we walked out of earshot.

The nurse wheeled me out of the hallway and into the next one. Past all the other locked doors and finally to my door. She used her passkey to unlock it and wheeled me in.

"Another nurse will be in shortly to tend to you." She said so softly, I almost couldn't hear her. "Do you need to use the lavatory?" She asked gently. When I shook my head in response, she helped me out of the chair and onto the side of the bed.

I sat on the side and took a few breaths. My body ached, as if phantom shocks were still coursing through my body. I felt as though all the strength in my body had been sucked out of me and I was nothing but a shell. So tired and sore from everything that had happened. I stared at the floor of the room until the door unlocked again and I looked up.

I noticed her small stature first and then her perfect grey hair, tied up in a neat bun. "Janice." The excitement in my tone was hard to hide.

She came into the room, setting down a tray of food and began attaching me to the fluid lines as she always did.

"Please, Janice." I sobbed. "You have to help me."

"I'm sorry dear." She stopped and placed her hand on my arm. "I can't help you." She turned and moved the food tray closer to me. "Eat up, dear. You're going to need your strength."

She squeezed my arm, firmly but not hard, twice.

My eyes met hers and she smiled at me, before leaving she tapped the food tray and then left the room. Closing the door behind her. I sat on the side of the bed for a moment longer, my hand tracing where hers had just been.

Two squeezes.

My eyes widened and I looked over at the food tray.

It seemed like any other normal meal I had been eating here. A soup bowl, two slices of buttered bread and a cup of water. Nothing looked out of the ordinary. I picked up the spoon and swished it around the lumpy brown soup. It knocked something at the bottom of the bowl. I scooped it up and when it surfaced, I saw it. Perched on the spoon was a passkey. The kind Dr Springer and the nurses use to get through the doors.

My heart raced. Janice had given me a passkey to help me escape.

Tears welled in my eyes, but I didn't let them fall. I was going to escape, and I was going to see Daniel and Luke again. I was going to make it to Illumina. I shoved the passkey under my pillow and I ate every last crumb of the food Janice had left me. I needed my strength. That was what she had told me. And she was right, because as soon as I had the chance, I was out of here.

~~~

A few hours had passed, and I was dozing off in bed when Dr Springer burst into my room. He was frantic and upset. I sat up as he entered and closed the door behind him.

"Things didn't go to plan in your test today." He said with flared nostrils. "Dr Gelch is not happy, and he wants answers." I looked at him confused. He paced at the end of my bed, pushing his glasses up his nose.

"What happened?" I dared to ask.

He stopped dead in his tracks at the foot of the bed and crossed his arms. "That is why I am here. I don't know what happened, it's only ever happened once before!" He yelled, glaring. I stayed silent. I had no clue what had happened either. But I had a feeling, telling him that would not end well.

"Tell me what you did!" He yelled. "Tell me now!" He stomped his foot like a child throwing a tantrum.

"I don't know what you're talking about." I said quietly.

"You almost broke my machine!" He was throwing a tantrum. "You did something while you were in the tub. Sophia had to stop the whole test to pull you out. This has only ever happened once, with another patient. But he's long gone." He was breathing heavily. "We never found out why it happened. Tell me what you did!"

"I don't know." I said again. I wasn't lying, I had no clue what he was talking about.

"Well, we will see if you feel the same when Dr Gelch sees you." He turned and stormed out of the room, shutting the door hard behind him.
~~~

I tried to remember what happened in the tub. But my memory was vague. I remembered being shoved under the water and surges of electricity flowing through my body and then nothing. Sophia pulled me out and I laid on the cold tiles, dripping wet. That's all that happened. All that I remember happening.

I stayed sitting on my bed and grabbed the passkey I'd hidden under my pillow. I held the small key and studied it. How could something so small, possibly be the key to my freedom? My gown didn't have pockets or anywhere for me to hide it. I felt my matted braid and shoved the key into the base of the braid against my head. It was thick enough to hold, as long as I didn't thrash my head around. I practiced turning my head either way, just to make sure it was secure and once I was convinced, I leaned back on the bed. Dr Gelch would be coming soon, no doubt to question me about the test. But I didn't have the answers he wanted.

The lock on the door sounded and it opened. I sat up quickly, bracing myself for whatever Dr Gelch was going to say or do. To my surprise, Janice slipped in and closed the door quickly.

"I don't have much time dear." She said as she hurried to my side. "Another nurse is going to escort you to Dr Gelch's office." She hurriedly unattached me from the fluid pumps and cords. "Here, drink this." She handed me a cup of water.

"Is this...?"

"Yes, yes." She interrupted and put the cup to my mouth. I guzzled down the water. "Good luck, dear."

I felt the stimulant rush through my veins, the fog clearing again and my vision focusing. "Thank you, Janice." I said and held her gaze.

The lock sounded and the door swung open. Sophia walked through the threshold.

"What are you doing?" She snapped at Janice.

"I was just assisting with getting this patient ready for transport." Janice hid the cup in her uniform pocket.

"I don't need help." She glared at Janice until the silence consumed the room. "Get out." Janice looked towards the floor as she passed by Sophia and left the room. She didn't stop to look back at me as the door closed behind her.

# Chapter 16

I followed Sophia down the hallway to the elevator. I needed to time this escape right, otherwise I'd be risking everything. I still didn't know the way out, so there was no point in trying right now.

Sophia swiped her passkey and pressed a button which illuminated immediately. My senses were heightened, I could hear and see everything clearly. I held onto the handrail to fake stabilising myself.

"Where are we going?" I asked, already knowing the answer.

Just as I thought, Sophia didn't answer. She kept her cruel stare forward.

The elevator was headed up levels and with each button that illuminated, I felt like I could taste fresh air. Freedom. The elevator came to a halt and the doors slid open. Sophia stood to the side and motioned with her hand for me to step out. I obliged and walked past her and out into a dim hallway. I turned, expecting Sophia to be standing beside me, when she wasn't there, I looked back into the elevator. The doors were now closing, with Sophia still inside.

She gave me a wicked grin and her face disappeared behind the steel doors.

I turned to face the dim hallway again and gulped hard. If Dr Gelch was going for an intimidating look, then it was certainly working. The hallway wasn't very long. It consisted of a beautiful hanging light in the centre of the ceiling. Which flickered orange and yellow shapes across the floor. There was a large mirror along one wall and a thin hallway table with a canvas sitting on top. Very minimalist. The canvas was a beautiful dark artwork. It was a mess of black and grey shapes, splattered across the white background. The end of the hallway opened into another room.

I took hesitant steps down the hallway, wary of who was waiting for me. When I reached the entrance, I peeped into the room and looked around in awe. It was a large room with dim lights to add to the ominous atmosphere. It looked like Dr Gelch had very expensive taste. A sizable deep blue lounge covered most of the floor. It curved around in an L-shape. A circular glass table in the centre and a beautiful rug, covered in shades of blue and green swirls. Massive artworks hung on the walls, in place of where I'd imagine windows would be. I took in the room and wondered if anything was ever touched. Everything was too clean, too perfect.

Dr Gelch cleared his throat and I jumped as he entered the room.

"Please, sit." He gestured to the dark couch and took up a spot for himself. He held a steaming cup and the smell of coffee, real coffee filled my nostrils.

I tentatively crossed the room and rounded the lounge. Choosing the furthest seat from Dr Gelch and sat uncomfortably. My body was tense and my mind was sharp. I noticed the way the light bounced off the objects surrounding us. The way the dimly lit lights flickered occasionally. Dr Gelch sipped from his brew and let out a long and irritated sigh. My eyes darted around the room, always coming back to his stare.

"Impressive. Isn't it." He chuckled. Motioning to the room around him. "It's the best I could do down here." He said proudly.

"Why are you doing this?" I asked, my eyes meeting his once more.

"Why am I doing this?" He repeated. Agitation laced his every word. "For the greater good, of course." He added. "You see, before the General won his little battle, some of the higher ups decided to use something from their arsenal. A dark plan to create enhanced soldiers, ensuring an easy win every time." He sipped loudly from his coffee.

"What do you mean?" I asked, keeping my voice low.

"A few select doctors, myself included, developed a new type of radiation. Once a soldier was exposed to it, they became unstoppable. They had heightened senses and doubled in muscle mass. They were quicker and more agile than any average human. But, with every experiment, there are complications." He rubbed the stubble on his chin, as if the failure was too hard to admit.

"The soldiers were volunteers in the beginning, you know. A large group of them came in to be enhanced. Their field training was going quicker than expected." He paused and gazed at me for a long time. Deciding if the information was too sensitive for my ears. "Well, the subjects weren't quite ready for battle, but we sent them out anyway. The only reason the General won the bloody war was because of us!" He yelled, "But do you think he thanked us? No, no he didn't. Because, like I said, there were complications. It was the first group of subjects to be enhanced. We had no idea what would happen after the first few weeks. Some of the soldiers turned savage and that's where it went wrong." He waved his hands in the air, "Lucky we won that war. But what we're doing down here will ensure a win every time. What's a few lives lost for the greater good?" I was speechless, I didn't even try to respond as I knew words would fail me. My mind ran over everything he had just told me, trying to piece it all together.

"Anyway," He said, shaking away the distant memory, drawing my attention back to him, "I am sure you know why you have been called to my quarters." He stated, not really a question. He waited silently for my response. The perfect interrogation technique to get me to talk. I nodded to confirm that I was aware of why I was here.

"So, tell me then." He leaned back on the lounge, making himself look comfortable. I did not mirror his relaxation and instead sat tall and on the edge of the lounge.

"I don't know what happened, sir." I said quietly.

He let out a loud laugh and leaned forward, spilling some of his coffee on the floor. I watched as the rug swallowed up the deep brown liquid like the desert sand after rain.

"Ha! You expect me to believe that?" He stood. I could feel the vibrations of his anger rising in his body. The pulse of his heart rate quickening. "I have never seen anything like it. Not once!" He yelled.

"I didn't *do* anything." I kept my voice calm and steady.

Dr Gelch took a few steps towards the artwork on the wall. He stood with his back towards me and I wondered for a split second if I could run. No, that wouldn't be smart. Not right now. I took a few deep breaths and smelt his odour. Not in a bad way. But I could smell his skin perspiring. My nostrils flared again and I took in the scent of his nervousness. I hadn't smelt that on him before.

He was frightened of me.

"You will tell me what happened in that tub. Or you will be put back in and not taken out." His voice was low. Then he turned to face me. His eyes filled with rage.

"Sir, please." I said calmly. "I am telling you the truth. I don't know what happened." When he didn't break his stare, I added. "I was put into the tub and hooked up. The next thing I remember, the nurse had dragged me out."

He blew air from his nostrils and huffed, storming towards me. He threw his coffee mug across the room and it shattered into pieces. I tensed my whole body, waiting for what was coming, but didn't move. Dr Gelch stopped at my feet and grabbed my neck with his hand. I didn't break my stare as he squeezed my neck hard and pulled me to my feet.

"You lying brat!" He yelled, through gritted teeth. He brought my face close enough to his that I felt his hot breath on mine. "There is something different about you. You aren't the same as the others and I am going to find out why. Even if that means cutting you open. Bit by bit." Whispering, his lips stroked my ear and I felt a shudder wave through me. "I won't let you ruin everything I have worked for!"

His free hand grasped the back of my head and my eyes widened as his fingers curled around the passkey hidden in my braid.

"Well, well, well. What is this then?" His voice was no more than a wicked whisper. He smirked in annoyance when he pulled the passkey out of my hair and squeezed it hard in the palm of his hand.

"I must have a traitor in my team." His laugh didn't hold any joy.

"Go...to...hell..." I managed to choke out.

He threw the passkey across the room and squeezed his other hand harder around my throat.

His eyes glowed with evil. Rage took him over and he threw me to the floor. I landed with such force that my wrist snapped on impact. I screamed loudly and held my arm. I turned to face him and he came down on me quickly. Hand wrapped around my throat again. My body shuddered once more.

And I felt my skin start to bubble. Only this time, I was in control and I was ready to let it out.

# Chapter 17

*Luke*

I followed Daniel down the tunnel. It was dark, only illuminated by an occasional dim light fixed to the wall. The yellow light was enough for us to see where we were headed. Even though I only had a very dull memory of escaping the lab before, this was definitely not the way I came.

"What's at the end of the tunnel?" I asked Daniel, barely more than a whisper.

"A door, leading to the elevator that connects the whole underground building." He said without so much as looking back at me.

It seemed to drag on for ages. Each dim yellow light buzzed as we passed it. The tunnel was damp and smelled of stale air. It didn't seem to be a path frequented.

"Who uses this entrance?" I asked.

"People like me. Anyone helping the lab. Or I have seen the *Snatchers* come through here sometimes." He spat out the name of the barbaric group as if he were any better than them.

"Right." I responded and I knew he could sense my tone.

A door came into view, lit up by a single yellow light, above a plain door in the centre of the wall. We both stayed silent as we crept closer. There weren't any guards on this side of the door. But I had no clue what was waiting on the other side. Daniel reached into his pocket and pulled out something small and silver. No bigger than a coin. I watched him as he straightened his stance and began walking towards the door.

"Stay against the wall." I could hear a nervous tone to his voice as he motioned for me to hide behind the door. "Don't move or say anything until I give you the all clear." He said.

He waved the small coin shaped object over the lock on the door and I realised that he had a key, a passkey. He really was one of them. Or at least, enough to be trusted with a key to the facility. I scoffed and shook my head in disbelief. Daniel shot me a look and I did as he said, backing up against the wall and keeping quiet. The door unlocked and Daniel opened it slightly.

My heart raced and I listened carefully as I heard Daniel greet the man on the other side. He was friendly enough with them, so they wouldn't suspect he was up to something. I heard a small amount of commotion and then silence.

"Coming?" Daniel peeped his head out and grinned at me.

I walked through the door and into a brightly lit room. The walls were the same white as I remembered. Clinical and depressing. A man lay leaning against the nearest wall, his head slumped over. I stepped over his outstretched legs and looked up at Daniel, who still wore the grin.

"You're enjoying this, aren't you?" I laughed.

He shrugged and continued to the elevator door. The plan was simple: plant a bomb on the lowest level of the lab and rescue Melody. The bomb was going to explode and take out each level. Seems simple enough. Except now we were here, we seemed awfully unprepared. Daniel checked in his backpack for the bomb he had made on our journey here. It was a tiny thing, no bigger than my forearm, but he said it was powerful. We would need to be well and truly out of the building before it went off. Daniel was going to plant the bomb and I was going to get Melody.

"Okay, you ready?" I said to Daniel.

He looked up at me and I saw what looked like fear in his eyes. "As I'll ever be." He turned to the elevator door. "Luke." He said, back still turned to me. "Just promise me, you will get her out."

"I promise." I placed a hand on his shoulder.

"Even if I am not out. If I don't make it. Get her the hell out of here and take her to Illumina."

I nodded. "I will, Daniel." I understood what he was really saying. "See you on the other side."

He swiped the passkey over the elevator door and we stepped in.

# Chapter 18

## *Melody*

*My body contorted in a familiar way. Instead of the pain I was so accustomed to, I felt relief. Like I had been holding back all the other times. The tests, although torture, had strengthened me in a way I hadn't realised. My skin finished its shift and I stood up, head held high. My torn hospital gown collapsed to the ground around me and I looked at the red headed man in front of me. The terror on his face might have been enough of a victory for me, but I needed more. With one effortless motion of my arm, I tossed him across the room. His plump body slammed into the wall, breaking the artwork under his force. He scrambled to get to his feet, and I was on him in an instant, pinning him back to the ground. The air was squeezed out of him as I leaned down on his chest.*

*"No! Please stop!" He screamed in a panic.*

*The sound of the fear in his voice sent shivers down my spine, feeding something deep and dark inside me. I bared my teeth and let out a terrible growl. I hovered over him, the smell of his panic filled the air. Large drops of saliva fell from my jagged mouth and covered his extended arm. I was going to take my time with this.*

"Please." *He pleaded.* "There's a cure. I can cure you!"

*I tilted my head and moved closer to him. My eyes widened. A cure? I thought, pulling away slightly.*

"Yes, yes! I can cure you." *He said as if he had read my expression.* "We created a cure six months ago. I can show you."

*How could I trust anything this vial human said? He tried to stand up, but I didn't move, blocking his way. I growled again and he pointed towards the far side of the room. My gaze followed his finger, and I saw a red door. My heart thumped in my chest. Maybe I could get him to cure me, then somehow kill him and escape, I thought.*

"Through that d-door, is the cure. I-I can take you." *He said, fumbling his words.*

*I moved my body from on top of him but kept my face close to his. I gestured with my head for him to move towards the door. He complied without any hesitation. Walking quickly towards the red door and with shaking hands, reached into his pocket for his passkey. I stood close to him, close enough that if he was to make one wrong move, it would be the last thing he did. He waved the key over the lock on the door and it clicked open. On the other side, was a dark staircase headed down.*

"Down the stairs, it leads to another room. That's where we keep the vials." *He pointed into the darkness.* "I would have to inject you." *He added.*

*I pushed him with my powerful arm and he stumbled down the first stair, catching himself on the handrail. I followed him closely,* to keep an eye on him, but I was also eager to find this cure and be done with shifting. The stairway was long and opened into a dark room. I couldn't see anything, even with my keen eyesight. The floor was concrete, I knew that much. And the foul smell that filled the air was almost enough to make me gag. Even in my creature form. Dr Gelch walked further into the room and stood to the side.

"I just need to turn the lights on." He said, pointing to a power box mounted on the wall.

The only tell that the power box was even there was a red flashing light. So small, I missed it coming down. I took a step closer to him, I didn't trust his intentions. But the hope that I could be cured was too strong.

"You stay there and I will turn the lights on. The vials are kept in a fridge on the other side." He said.

He waited for my approval before walking slowly towards the power box, he didn't turn his back to me and for good reason too. He felt for the wall with his hand and when he reached the box he turned to face it. I tried to look at what he was doing, but it was too dark. This felt wrong. Something wasn't right. Then he pulled a large lever that sounded some sort of generator. The lights flickered and I saw a flash of white light. Then another and I shook my head and blinked rapidly, because I think I just saw...

"Kill her!" Dr Gelch ordered and sprinted back up the stairs too quick for me to register.

The bright lights turned on and I squinted as I turned to face the room again. Lines and lines of creatures stood in front of me.

All still like statues and all wearing helmets.

The same helmets I was forced to wear during my tests.

I planted my feet firmly to the ground and sized them up. They had all been brutally disfigured and I wondered if that was from the torture they had endure here. Dr Gelch had created an army of creatures. In unison, they turned to face me. Growls and snarls came from a few of them and I braced myself for what might be my last fight.

# Chapter 19



*Luke*


The elevator door opened and everything went into slow motion. Daniel walked out first, greeting the two guards standing in the hallway. He held a hand sized weapon behind his back. I kept my head down and stayed a good few paces behind him. When they questioned why he was on that level he brought the little weapon to the first guard's necks and the man stilled, eyes rolling back. The weapon was small, but man it was effective. The first guard was down in a matter of moments. The second guard raised his baton and charged for Daniel. I intercepted just in time with my own sword. It sliced through the guard's baton with ease and he stepped back, clenching his fists. I sheathed my sword and he began swinging his fists. I laughed as he swung one after the other, dodging all of them. I then gave him a few strikes myself, each one landing. With the last blow, my closed fist made contact with his jaw and his body flew backwards, falling limp to the floor.

"Nice one." Daniel encouraged me.

"You too." I smiled back.

"I need to do something on this level." Daniel motioned to the end of the hallway. "You go find Mel and meet back at the tunnel. I will set the bomb off in one hour." I nodded in understanding and walked back to the elevator. "Wait." Daniel stopped me. "You'll need this." He handed me the passkey.

"See you up top." I said. I waved the passkey over the elevator door and walked in.

The doors closed slowly, Daniel remained still and smiling.

I pressed the level where I remembered the rooms were and unsheathed my sword again. I gripped the handle tightly and took a few deep breaths. I prepared myself for whatever I would find on the way to Melody. Nothing would stop me from getting to her. I had to be quick, someone would set off the alarm as soon as they saw me. Every floor that I passed felt like my heart thumping in my body. Closer and closer to Melody.

The elevator doors opened and I looked into the empty hallway. It was just as I remember it. Clinical white walls, fluorescent white lights and door after door of prisoners held captive. I slowly entered the hallway and looked either way to see if anyone was there.

No one, not even a nurse.

I walked quickly to the first door, checking the details on the file mounted there. The patient's name had been replaced with a number, but there was a picture at the top. A young boy, no more than twelve years old. He had dark hair, hanging straight and his eyes were surrounded by dark circles. I stared into the eyes on the picture and felt his pain. His sadness. I felt a lump form in my throat and cleared it before tears formed. I had to remember why I was here.

I am here for Melody.

I moved onto the next door. Same file layout, with different numbers and pictures. This one was of an elderly man, he too had the same sad expression as the boy. I moved to the next door, each brutalised face sadder than the last. Then I stopped dead in my tracks.

"Patient M2605. Melody." I whispered as I stared at her photo. Her beautiful blonde hair. Usually tied up tightly into a braid, had bits falling around her face. Her piercing blue eyes looked straight through me, with a fierce expression. A death promise to the person holding her captive. I looked up at her door and found the passkey in my pocket. I held on to the door handle, hesitating for a moment. Unsure of what I might be faced with on the other side. I took a deep breath and unlocked the door. I opened it and stepped in.

She wasn't here.

The blood in my veins boiled. They must have taken her to do a test right now. I walked further into the room and looked around hurriedly. I needed a clue of where she might have been taken. I found nothing of interest, some clean sheets, medical supplies and a few charts from her machines. I heard commotion in the hallway. Nurses were chatting to one another and I hid crouched on the other side of the bed. I couldn't make out what they were saying, but they were getting closer.

The door unlocked and began to open.

# Chapter 20



*Daniel*

I watched Luke as he entered the elevator and I smiled at him. He knew I wasn't planning on meeting him in the tunnel and he hadn't said anything. He was good, I could tell. I knew he would be able to find Mel and get her out. I saw the way he looked at her on the first day I met him.

I had been trying to figure out a way out of the city for the last few months. Once I realised Mel was shifting, I knew I had to get us out. But I had ties to the lab. They had approached me after our father was killed and asked me to help them with some weapons. In exchange, they would offer assistance whenever we needed. At the time, I was so angry that my father was killed, I was more than happy to see the creatures locked away down here. So, I made gadgets and weapons and if we were ever short on food or water, they would supply it to us. I was hiding a stash of food and supplies, big enough for us to start again somewhere else. Planning our escape. Then Luke showed up and it was the perfect plan. The things I had seen down here, the things I myself had done, would haunt me for the rest of my life. And to know that they had my sister made my stomach twist in ways it never had before. She had taken care of me when our mother couldn't. Mel had looked out for me my whole life really. So, it was time to repay her. To repay every poor soul trapped here.

I hadn't told Luke the full extent of my plan, because I knew he wouldn't agree. I turned and walked to the end of the corridor and slipped into the control room. The man sitting on the chair didn't have time to react as I pushed my device into his neck. It was a small box, inside were two different vials of drugs. When I pushed the button on the device, it sent both drugs through the needle at the end and into the subject. The drugs, when mixed together, were deadly. The lab wanted a strong sedative, able to be injected easily into the creatures. This was one of the first prototypes. I worked on the dosage with the lab chemist over the course of a few weeks to perfect it. The man slumped in the chair before he even knew I was there. I pushed him to the floor and took up his seat.

I looked up at the screens and hundreds of buttons on the switch board in front of me. I had to remember how to unlock all the doors safely. I looked at the security screens, searching for Mel. The security screens mainly watched the test rooms, some of the hallways and some of the staff areas. I couldn't see her in any of the test room screens. So, it was safe to assume she was in her room. There were multiple tests taking place right now. A woman in the cage, in the depths of the lab. She was screaming as she shifted back and forth. The tub room was empty, which I thought was odd. Since Dr Springer loved to use that torture device often. He wanted me to invent a machine that would hold the patient in between shifts. Right on the cusp of shifting and then bring them back. He said it would help with his work, but deep down, I knew he just loved to torture them. Weaken them. I shook the thought out of my mind. I had created so many torture devices. Now it was time to shut it all down.

I began pressing buttons on the switch board. Only specific ones that would turn off the power in the test rooms. I had created a secret code that would turn them off when overridden.

One by one, the torture rooms turned dark and the murmurs of the staff filled the speakers. A few voices came over the radio attached to the man laying on the floor. I had to respond quickly and try to avoid chaos.

"Control room here." I said in a fake voice. "Something happened to the switch board. Fixing it now." I said confidently.

A few more murmurs and some profanity came through the radio again but I ignored it. Time for the next part to my plan. Unlocking all the patient doors. I just hoped that Luke had found Mel already.

# Chapter 21

*Luke*

The door didn't open all the way and instead just lingered. I waited for a moment longer before walking around the bed and standing behind the door. I listened and peeked around into the hallway. It seemed like I wasn't the only one confused by this breach. Some of the other patients were doing exactly as I was. Each one of them wore a shocked and scared look upon their faces.

Some patients had been waiting for this moment for a long time and they burst into the hallway like rabid animals. The nurses began yelling and scrambling down the hallway. One of them pushed a big red button on the wall and all the lights switched to crimson. A siren sounded and the patients started running in every direction. One of the nurses tried to get into the elevator but she was ripped out by a few of the patients. She screamed as they ripped at her clothes and face. The other nurse used the distraction to her advantage and escaped into the elevator, the doors closing her in. The patients tore apart the nurse on the ground with their bare hands.

Blood spilled from her torso and her screams ceased as death greeted her. I walked into the hallway, sword still drawn. Each patient I passed stepped aside, as if they knew I was one of them. As if they could see that I too had been tortured as they had. I looked out of place in this white landscape. Wearing my black combat gear and wielding a weapon sharp enough to slice through bone. The sirens were so loud, beaming over again. Some of the patients screamed in unison with the siren. Clutching their ears and falling to the ground. I knew their pain. I had been here, in their shoes. I had to get them all out. I stopped at the end of the hallway and looked in the room to my left. The little boy was hiding under the bed, eyes squeezed shut. I walked into his room and crouched beside the bed. He looked up at me, terror filling his eyes.

I knew he wouldn't be able to hear my voice over the siren, but I spoke anyway.

"I am going to help you." I yelled. "Come with me." I stretched out my arms and he did the same. He gripped his arms tightly around my neck and I hoisted him up.

Bringing him into the chaos of the hallway, I walked past all of it and straight to the elevator. I waved the passkey over the lock on the elevator and it flashed red. I tried again and again. Holding the boy to my body, I looked around for another way out. The elevator must have been shut down when the alarm was pushed. The hallway was lit up red and the patients crawled and stumbled around like zombies. At the other end of the hallway, a door was slightly ajar.

I squinted my eyes to see a woman on the other side. She motioned for me to come towards her. I was hesitant, but at this point, what other choice did I have?

I stepped over the corpse of the nurse splayed out on the floor. Mindful to turn the boy's head away. Though I know he had probably seen much worse, done much worse. Holding my sword tightly I walked the length of the hallway to the open door. It was dark on the other side. I tensed and placed the boy down behind me. He gripped my leg tightly and stayed close. I used my sword to open the door and on the other side, was an elderly woman with her hands up in surrender. I searched behind her, wondering if this was a trap. But the room behind her was empty. I stepped in with the boy and closed the door behind me. The lights flashed red as the siren continued and the woman's face was illuminated with each flicker.

"Who are you?" I said in a rough voice. My sword outstretched between us.

"My name is Janice." She replied in a sweet, but frightened voice. "I am one of the nurses, but I want to help you."

She felt familiar when I studied her face. "Do I know you?" I asked.

She took a step closer and I backed away. "You might, dear. I have nursed a lot of people in my time."

"How can I trust you?" I couldn't shake the feeling that I knew her, somehow.

"I understand your worry. But you will just have to believe it when I say that I am on your side." She slowly put her hands down and smiled sweetly. "What can I do to help?"

I nodded, still cautious but something within me told me to trust her. "Get these patients out of here. That's what you can do." I passed the boy to her. He was either too drugged up to care or still in a state of terror. But he walked over to her and clung to her arm. His eyes were dark and glassy.

"The elevator will be locked from the alarm." Janice said quietly. "But there is a stairwell. I can use that to get them out."

"A stairwell?"

"Yes, dear. There is a stairwell that leads to a back exit." She nodded and pointed to the back of the room.

I vaguely remember taking the stairs when I escaped. Dr Osbourn showed them to me.

"Do the stairs lead out to the city?" My question came out harsher than intended.

"Yes. Yes, they lead out to the city through an underground tunnel system. The guards aren't posted there because the door is always locked and no one uses the tunnels." She said, leaning in close.

I thought about her words carefully. "Can you get the patients out?" I asked.

"I can try." She straightened and held her chin high. Like she had been waiting for this moment for a long time.

# Chapter 22

## *Melody*

The creatures stalked towards me with snarls and bared teeth. They snapped at one another as they stood shoulder to shoulder, edging closer. My feet were planted firmly and I could feel each footstep they took vibrate through the ground. I spread my toes and braced myself. I wasn't going down without a fight. The first creature came at me quickly, yet clumsily and I knocked it from its feet with an effortless blow to the stomach. The creature landed with a thud and tripped the next creature over. They stumbled and scrambled to their feet.

Not very smart then, I thought to myself.

Instinct took over and the animal inside me knew what to do. Each creature that stood forward was defeated within a matter of moments. I took a few blows, but nothing that shook me. The next creature stepped forwards, gnashing its teeth. It lunged and I ducked just in time, using all four of my limbs to be as agile as I could. These creatures were no different from me. All brought here against their will and turned into monsters. They had all been tortured and held captive. Even in my creature form, my heart broke for them. With each creature that fell, a small thread of guilt washed over me. A creature lunged forward again and I shot into the air, gripping the creature's shoulders and swung myself over the top of it. Behind it now, I grabbed its head and with all my strength, ripped it clean from its body. The head and helmet rolled across the floor. Its huge, disfigured body collapsed to the ground. I turned to face the rest of them, still snapping at the air and growling at me as they closed the distance between us.

The helmet detached from the severed head and an orange light flashed on the top of it. The creature's head came to a halt and golden eyes stared back at me.

I looked up at the other creatures, whose eyes were as black as coal.

Then, I had an idea.

# Chapter 23

*Luke*

Janice did a great job of rounding up as many patients as she could and hurrying them down a long and dark passage. She said it led out to the staircase they would take. I didn't know why, but I felt like I could trust her.

"Do you know where this patient is?" I asked between the line of patients. I held Melody's file up and pointed to her picture.

Her eyes widened and she nodded. "Yes, M2605. She was taken to Dr Gelch's office."

My heart dropped. "I need to get to her now!" I yelled at Janice.

"Go! Go!" She shooed me off, as if she knew how critical it was that I got to her.

"Get them all out, then get out yourself!" I yelled over my shoulder as I took off down the passageway. Carefully weaving through the stumbling patients as I hurried to the stair-case.

I had been to Dr Gelch's office a few times when I was a prisoner here. After the tests had gone wrong. They had questioned me and accused me of things during the tests. I had broken several of their machines and no one knew why, not even me. I had blood tests and whole-body scans done to figure out what was going on. The results were always inconclusive. Dr Gelch was not a nice man, and the thought of Melody being alone with him was unbearable.

When I made it to the stairs, I ushered some of the patients downward as I began my ascent. I climbed the steps two at a time. Controlling my breathing and trying to keep pace. There was a long way to go. Dr Gelch's office was almost at the top. My mind was racing with all of the possibilities of what might be happening with Melody right now. Was she being interrogated? Was Dr Gelch harming her? Praising her? I had no way of knowing. It fuelled me as I quickened my steps, careful not to slip and send myself tumbling back down. When I reached the platform of Gelch's office I stopped at the door, panting heavily. I withdrew my sword and approached the door, listening intensely. It was silent. I carefully gripped the door handle and twisted the knob. It was locked, of course. So much for sneaking in.

I reared up and kicked the door with all my force. The door flew off its hinges and crashed to the floor. Dr Gelch would've heard that and my sneak attack was ruined. I hurried in and rushed down the dim hallway. The elevator door was stuck open. I looked in quickly, but it was empty. My heart pounded as I looked around the room for Melody, or Dr Gelch, or anyone. The room seemed empty. I let out a sharp huff. Feeling defeated and wondering where the hell he would've taken her.

Then I heard it.

The growls and snarls coming from somewhere close. The hair on my neck stood on its end as I turned towards the sound. A red door on the far side of the room was open slightly. Another growl sounded and I ran for the door.

*"Melody?"* I pushed through my mind.

I stopped at the threshold and gripped my sword tightly. I took a few deep breaths to steady myself, before taking the stairs slowly. Listening to the roaring sounds of creatures below.

*"Melody, I am here."* I pushed again. But there was no answer.

There was a bright light at the bottom of the stairs and it looked like it opened up into a room. I kept to the wall and took each step quietly and slowly as I neared the entrance.

When I got to the bottom, my jaw almost fell to the floor. There she was. Not the damsel in distress I had imagined. But a warrior in her creature form, tearing through a swarm of other creatures. Bodies of the fallen were sprawled across the floor. Some were dead, beheaded or without limbs. But the ones left standing seemed concussed or confused. Melody was ripping their helmets from their heads and smashing them.

I took a step closer and she turned to face me. Her eyes went wild in a frenzy. She snarled loudly in my direction and

I sheathed my weapon. Holding my hands up in surrender, I took another two steps closer. She dropped a helmet from her mouth and released the dazed creature. Then came down on all fours, growling low again.

*"Melody, it's me. It's Luke."*

I stood still as she came closer to me. Her sheer size was enough to send any smart man running. But when I stared at her, all I saw were her beautiful blue eyes. I had many dreams about her eyes. The different shades of blue speckled through them and the dark ring surrounding her pupil. They reminded me of the ocean. She stared back at me. Only inches from my face.

*"Luke."* Her voice caressed the back of my mind in a whisper and my throat caught as I held back tears.

She took a few steps closer to me and as she did, she began to shift.

# Chapter 24

### *Melody*

Luke caught me in his arms as I collapsed. My human form felt weak and unnatural. I looked up at him and took in each of his features. Studying his face. His dark brown eyes stared back at me and I swear he had tears welling. His pitch-black curls framed his beautiful face. And his bushy eyebrows were drawn together as he searched my face for answers.

"You came for me." I said.

He clasped my face, gently brushing a tear from my cheek. We stared at each other as the world moved slowly around us. His face was so close, our breath intertwined. I brought my hand up, behind his head.

Curling my fingers through his shaggy hair and I pulled him in. Our lips came crashing together and I kissed him passionately but gently.

He kissed me back, like he had been waiting for eternity to do so.

He held me close as we kissed and it felt like the world beyond us stopped. We pulled away only enough to look into each other's eyes and he smiled.

"I have been wanting to do that since the day I met you." He said and wiped another tear from my face.

I felt my cheeks blush and I knew he noticed. A low grumble sounded behind us and I jolted back to reality. Suddenly realising that I was standing there naked. I covered myself with my arms and Luke looked away. He found an old sheet curled up in the corner of the room. It was dirty, but it would have to do for now. I wrapped it around myself and turned to face what was left of the army of creatures.

"I removed the helmets." I said to Luke. Who was standing between me and the creatures. "It seems to be some sort of mind control." I added.

"And now they won't hurt us?" He asked, tense.

"I don't know about that. But it stopped them from attacking me."

I stepped closer to the creatures. Their human eyes filled with terror. They seemed more docile now, most of them confused, like they had just awakened from a trance. I turned to face Luke quickly.

"Do you think you can talk to them? Through your mind?" I asked.

"What?" He laughed. "It's only ever worked with you." He added when I didn't reply.

"If you could reach them, they might be able to help us." I explained.

The creatures wandered around the room and mostly kept to themselves as Luke and I talked and tried to come up with an escape plan. He told me that Daniel was here too and that he was going to set off a bomb, anytime now. We needed to get out soon.

"I think we will be quicker in our creature forms and if there is any chance of me getting through to this lot." He pointed to the remaining three creatures in the room. "Then I will have to shift." He began to remove his weapons and clothes.

"Okay. Let's do it." I held out my hand and Luke interlaced his finger with mine. "Together."

"Together." He repeated.

I closed my eyes and began to shift.

*Luke let go of my hand and watched me change form. I moved forward into the room to catch the attention of the other creatures. The three of them stood from where they were and walked closer. Luke came up beside me, he had shifted into his creature form and I gave him a nod.*

*He walked forward letting a gentle growl rumble through his throat and the three creatures bowed their heads slightly, in submission.*

*"We need your help." He spoke through his mind.*

*The other creatures straightened their posture, eyes wide.*

*They had heard him.*

# Chapter 25

*Daniel*

The alarm had been set off. I didn't have much time. I finished attaching the fuse and wires across the control board. I didn't want any part of this building surviving our attack. I connected the last wire and stepped back to look at my work. Explosives carefully laid out across the entire control board. When the bomb went off, I wanted the whole building to burn with it. So, I needed a fail safe, in case the bomb didn't reach the upper levels.

Satisfied with my work, I flung my backpack back on and ran from the room into the hallway. The red flashes from the alarm disorientated me slightly, but I held a hand on the wall as I walked to steady myself. The sound from the alarm was deafening, piercing through my eardrums and echoed through my head. I had to get to the lowest level so I could set the bomb. I reached the elevator and searched in my pocket for the passkey. Swearing to myself when I remembered that I gave it to Luke. I stood at the elevator door for a moment before realising the elevator wouldn't be working while the alarm sounded. I knew of a hidden door that led to a back staircase, so I made a run for it. Not many people knew this was here but I had stumbled across the blueprints of the building during one of my first meetings with Dr Gelch.

I stood at the top of the stairs and stared down into the dark abyss. I gulped hard and began my descent, knowing I had a long way to go before I reached the bottom. I had only heard rumours about what they kept on the lowest level. But if any of that was remotely true, I'd have to be very careful. I felt in my bag for the other weapons I packed. The small handheld injection device (S.H.I.D as I liked to call it), a fighting knife, the bomb I had made and a few other inventions I thought might come in handy. Not much, but maybe just enough to get me in and out. If I didn't run into much trouble.

I wasn't very good with combat, Luke made that blatantly obvious when we sparred in the forest. But if I could catch them off guard and use my weapons, then I would be fine.

I hurried each step, careful not to tumble all the way down. Although that might be quicker, I'd probably end up a pile of mush. I passed the level for Dr Gelch's office and stopped briefly when I noticed the door had been knocked off its hinges. I didn't linger and kept heading down. I knew the types of things he did to his prisoners. So I wouldn't be surprised at all if they had sought revenge when their room doors unlocked.

My head was becoming dizzy from the tight rectangle I was moving in. Down and around. The air was getting stale and I knew I was getting close. The concrete walls leaking water from small imperfections cracked through them. I heard whispers and voices as I slowed my steps. The red flashing light from the alarm was illuminating one of the walls every other second. When I got closer, I noticed an old nurse, ushering patients into the staircase and down the stairs. I crept around the final corner, and she stopped when she saw me.

"It's okay, I am on your side." I said, hands up in surrender.

She silently kept ushering the patients and stepped closer to me.

"Are you here alone?" She asked, raising an eyebrow at me.

"No, I came here with a friend. Luke." I said and she released a breath. "We're getting my sister out."

She nodded and asked. "What is your plan then?"

"I am going to blow it all up." I said, looking behind her at the last of the patients to follow the line into the darkness of the stairs. "Get everyone out." I added.

She nodded and hurried after the patients, yelling out at them to keep going and get to the bottom.

"You're going to the bottom?" I asked, catching up to her.

"Yes, there is a secret door that leads to underground tunnels. I'll get them out to the city through them."

"Aren't the cells down there?" I asked worriedly.

"You certainly know your way around, sir." She eyed me cautiously.

"I used to work for Dr Gelch." Shame filled my voice. "Before everything happened."

She squeezed my arm as if she understood what it meant to be bound to Dr Gelch unwillingly.

"At the bottom, it comes to a flat level. There are two doors. The one to the left leads to the tunnels and out to the city. The one on the right leads to the cells." She spoke so softly.

I nodded and we continued downwards. We made it to the bottom level and I wasn't surprised when I found the door to the cells locked.

The elderly nurse disappeared through the ocean of patients gathered around the bottom of the stairs. With a loud bang, the people started to move. Out the door and into the dark tunnel. She told them of places to hide once they made it to the city and that she would come find them and tend to them while they detoxed from the drugs still flowing through their veins. I admired her courage.

I dropped to one knee and pulled my bag in front of me, unzipping it and searching inside. I packed a few things other than my weapons, for this exact reason. I rummaged through the pockets until I found it.

"Yes!" I said excitedly. My voice echoed back up the eerie staircase.

"Are you coming out too?" The nurse was at my side.

"No actually." I looked up at her. "I am going in there." I nodded towards the door to the right.

"What on earth for?" She spat out.

"I am going to set the bomb off in there." I stood and walked over to the door.

I fiddled with the handle for a moment and then used my makeshift key. It was an invention of mine made from tiny metal balls, attached to each other on a string. The string was tied around a piece of metal like a bike chain. The balls were able to move through the keyhole and morph into the shape the key should be. Unlocking any door.

The nurse stood closely behind me, watching my every move. The lock clicked and I opened the door. The stench of rotting flesh and moisture hit me like a brick wall. I coughed and held my hand to my nose.

"That's pungent." I said to the nurse.

"I am sure no one comes down here. This door hasn't been opened in a long time."

I stepped through the threshold and into the pitch-black room. I could feel something watching me. The hair on my neck stood on its end and I heard shuffling around the room. But nothing came into the light.

# Chapter 26

### *Melody*

We walked up the stairs and out into Dr Gelch's lounge area. The alarm had been set off and was flashing red every other second. Luke went through the door first, closely trailed by me and the three other creatures. They weren't able to communicate like we could, but they understood and that was enough. The smaller creature, a male, carried Luke's bag, with his weapons and his clothes. That creature was deformed enough that he wouldn't be much use in a fight. So he kept to the back and seemed more than happy to be a porter for the group. The other two were much bigger, bigger than me and were covered in muscles. One was a male and the other a female. They snapped and gnashed their teeth at one another occasionally, like for a brief moment they forgot who they were and turned feral. It must have been hard for them to readjust. But we needed them, needed each other to get out.

*The stench of fear filled the room. I knew Dr Gelch was hiding somewhere. The five of us took up a V formation, like birds that have taken flight, with Luke as the leader. Luke sniffed high into the air. He nodded at the two hulking creatures and they fanned out, slowly stalking the scent. It didn't take long for the male to hunt down the doctor. He had hidden himself in a cupboard on the far wall. Dr Gelch's pleas fell on deaf ears, as he was dragged across the floor by his ankle. He was trying to wiggle free from the tight grip of the creature.*

"Please!" He begged. "Please, just let me go and I won't tell anyone what happened here."

*Although he tried to sound sincere, there was a hint of disdain in his voice that couldn't be ignored. The male creature lifted Dr Gelch's overweight body from the ground, his shirt untucking from his pants, revealing an orange trail of hair leading to his navel. Blood rushed to his face and he scowled and spat on the floor.*

"You rotten creatures." He huffed. "You will all die. You are nothing without this lab. Nothing!"

*"Do you want the honours, or shall I?" Luke stroked my mind with his voice.*

*"Be my guest." I responded and turned to face the hallway. "I have someone else I need to pay a visit to."*

*Luke and I agreed to meet at the tunnel in fifteen minutes. The elevators weren't working, so Luke told me of the stairwell I needed to use. Luke and the giant male creature stayed back to deal with Dr Gelch. I trusted Luke to end his life, while I sorted out my own revenge. I brought the other two creatures with me.*

*"Be careful." Luke nuzzled me with his strong head and I pushed into him in response.*

*"See you soon." I replied and took off towards the stairs.*

*We took the stairs and quickly searched every level. All we found were empty rooms and corpses of the staff and patients. We stopped on the level I knew the most, where the patients were kept. When I saw the rooms empty and hallways deserted, I hoped they had escaped. I was glad to see that most had escaped. Only a few bodies lay in the hallway. I had almost given up when I heard the faintest whispering. My keen ears pricked when I recognised his voice. A deep growl sounded from inside my body and the other two creatures perked up, holding a defensive stance either side of me. My skin bubbled and my bones snapped as I shifted back into my human form.*

I fell to my knees, naked and panting. The small male creature dumped Lukes' combat clothes on the ground next to me and I quickly pulled them on. I wanted to face Dr Springer this way, in my human form. We stalked down the hallway and through the door opposite the elevator. The creatures both kept close behind me. The red flashes from the alarm still pulsed as we neared the end of the second hallway. The hallway that led to the room with the tub. I gulped hard at the memory that surfaced, reaching for two enormous friends I had trailing behind me. Dr Springer could not hurt me today. The whispering stopped as we stood at the door to the viewing room.

*"Open it, please."* I pushed through my mind.

The bigger female creature was more than happy to oblige and punched the door right off its hinges. It broke in two and smashed to the floor. Dr Springer let out a hoarse yell and ducked behind a chair. The creature stood back and allowed me to enter.

"*Thank you.*" I said bowing my head slightly. She did the same.

"Hello Dr Springer." I said as I entered the small viewing room. It consisted of a study desk with a computer and chair. A large one-way window to watch the subject in the tub and a few other machines on the walls. "I am so glad we found you."

"This is all your doing!" He yelled over the back of the chair. "I knew it was you. I knew you did something! You will pay for this."

I saw movement in the corner of my eye and recognised the long dark hair before anything else. Sophia took a step forward from where she was and smiled at me. That same wicked smile she wore while I was being tortured.

# Chapter 27

*Daniel*

I found the flashlight I'd packed in my bag and clicked it on. The light illuminated a small circle on the wall. The dark cell was damp and smelled like food that had been left to rot. The nurse stayed close behind me, one of her hands firmly clutched onto the back of my belt. I wasn't sure if she was scared, or if she was going to drag me out by my pants. But either way, the reassurance she was there made me feel a little better. Sweat droplets formed on my forehead as I used the torch to light the way. It wasn't a very good torch, only illuminating a small circle. I traced the wall with the torch and slowly took in the huge cell.

"I thought there were multiple cells?" I said to the nurse.

"I don't know much about this place." She said, barely a whisper.

The walls were as dark as night and covered in leaky cracks. The stench was enough to make me cover my nose. The floor was flat and looked like it was in the shape of a large rectangle. There were bones as white as paper scattered around. No flesh left at all. The nurse and I took slow steps as we searched the room. Still hearing the occasional shuffle or movement. I stopped the torch over a chain hanging on the wall and nudged the nurse to look. We walked over carefully and noticed the shackles it was attached to. There were four chains. Two hanging high on the wall and two on the ground. They looked like something you would bind a very dangerous prisoner with. I gulped hard as we both realised the shackles had been broken and not unlocked. There was a noise behind us, like something being dragged along the floor.

We turned slowly, the torch lighting the way.

I stood still, the torch stopped on the disfigured man in front of us. His eyes had been torn from their sockets and only dark bloodied holes remained. His bald head reflected the light. One of his arms was deformed from a mutation that didn't make sense.

It hung low, dragging along the ground. The skin on that arm was green and black, with huge veins popping out. Long jagged fingernails stuck out the end of his dangly fingers. The rest of his body looked human, except for the black veins that ran under his skin. He wore grey linen pants, torn at the knees and covered in filth. The nurse gasped from behind me and took a step towards him.

"Wait." I said, but she pushed past me.

"Greg?" She asked. The man sniffed the air and made a grunting noise. "Greg, it's me, Janice." She reached her hands out and I would have stopped her, but the man responded.

"J-Jan..." He huffed. "Jan-ince?"

I lifted a brow in confusion. The old nurse held her hands out and he reached for her, they grasped each other and she began to cry.

"Oh Greg." She sobbed. "How could they do this to you?" He held her with his human arm and they both dropped to the floor.

"Can someone tell me what's going on?" I asked.

"My name..." The man started, his voice coarse from disuse. "I am Dr Greg Osbourn." He held his chin high.

"Greg was one of the top research doctors in the city. It's why Dr Gelch asked him to be a part of *a new experiment*, one that would *change the world*. How could he say no to all the promises he was given. Until he realised what Dr Gelch was really doing." The nurse, Janice, began. "Dr Gelch told Greg that it was all to find a cure, to help with a top-secret illness. Greg didn't know what he was really doing then. He had created enhanced soldiers for the General, but once that backfired on him, he dove into the depths of hell itself and created monsters. They took samples from the creatures who had been affected after the explosion and mixed their blood with humans who weren't mutated. Dr Gelch realised how much power he had and began torturing the creatures to find new information, new strengths. He was power hungry and his moral compass was nowhere to be seen. Greg found out and didn't agree. So, he helped a few patients escape."

"Luke..." I whispered.

"Dr Gelch found out and he took my Greg." She held on to the mutated man and sobbed into his chest. "Dr Gelch locked Greg up for betraying him and made me work on the nursing team to earn Greg's freedom. But I didn't know where he took you. Or that he had done this." She cried and the man held her. "I would have come, Greg."

He was weak, sick. His skin was pale and the black veins that flowed under it moved, like they had life of their own.

"Dr Osbourn?" I asked and he lifted his head. The gruesome holes where his eyes should be stared through my soul. "What happened to you?"

"Experi...ments." He rolled his shoulders. "Gone... wrong."

I nodded and told him of my plan, to bring the whole lab down. He smiled when I told him there were other people here with me and that we had already managed to get most of the patients out.

~~~

"Okay, I need to get this bomb set and we need to get the hell out of here!" I said as I finished attaching the final wires.

Janice and Dr Osbourn whispered to each other, still cradling each other on the floor.

"Okay, lovebirds. Time to go." I moved closer to them.

Janice stood, her face grave, "We aren't going."

"We have to."

"Greg won't make it, he's too weak. His mutation is killing him." She turned and faced her husband. "I won't leave him." Tears welled in her eyes again. "Not again."
~~~

"Janice, you will die." I reached out for her. "Both of you will die!"

"I... am already... dying." Dr Osbourn rasped.

She leaned in, close to my ear and whispered, "I have been working for *that* man, in hopes he would free my Greg. But I didn't know that my husband was below me this whole time. Being tortured." She sobbed again.

"Janice."

She put her hand up to stop me speaking. "Show me how to use this gadget, then I want you gone." Her voice didn't waver.

I felt guilty for not putting up more of a fight. Instead, I nodded slowly and showed her how to arm the bomb.

# Chapter 28

*Luke*

The strong creature held Dr Gelch's wriggling body up high in the air. The creature was huge. Much bigger than me and covered in dark muscles. Although he listened to me, he had this wildness about him that I knew I could use to my advantage.

This creature remembered who Dr Gelch was and what he had done to us. The doctor had almost lost consciousness from being upside down for so long.

"Put him on the ground." I commanded my new friend.

And he did so immediately. Dropping the red-haired man to the floor with a thud. Dr Gelch groaned as he rolled over and sat up.

"Who are you?" Dr Gelch looked at me with amazement across his face.

A low warning sounded from the throat of my new friend as if he sensed the threat Dr Gelch once posed to me. I knew the creature would protect me, if I needed him to. I told the creature what I was going to do with Dr Gelch, and that I wanted to be the one to kill him. The creature growled and snarled in understanding and kept a close eye on the man while I circled like a shark.

Dr Gelch gasped and his eyes widened, his gaze darted between us, as if he was somehow trying to read our minds. He scrambled on the floor, but the creature held him in place with one snarl.

"I don't believe it." He panted, lower lip quivering. "You're an Alpha! You can communicate with the other creatures!" He pointed his short, fat finger at me, and his hand shook with fear.

Alpha? I thought to myself.

"We have been studying the creatures for a long time. Some doctors had theories that there might be an Alpha. There always is in the animal kingdom." His voice was stunned, as if he wasn't a believer until now. "I wonder..." His voice trailed off as he thought intensely.

It would make sense why I could always hear the other creatures when they wanted to communicate with me. Oscar, Melody and these new friends. Even though they couldn't all speak to me, I could speak to them. And they followed my command without hesitation.

I rose up on to my sturdy legs and let out a growl. One that I had been holding in this whole time, pushing all my anger and frustration into it. My sound shook the building, the vibrations sending a shockwave through the floor.

I was done with this man. With his torture and malicious ideas. He trembled as I stalked closer to him. Sweat dripped from his brow. The creature stepped up behind him, to make sure he *couldn't escape. Couldn't try to run while I destroy him, piece by piece. I knew I didn't have much time until the bomb went off, but I would take as long as I could with this. Savouring every moment of his terror.*

*I lunged forward and he screamed.*

# Chapter 29



*Melody*

"Sophia." I said roughly.

And she took a step closer to me. The nurse held her wicked smile as she twisted her arm and the skin began to bubble. I watched in shock as her arm became a lethal weapon. The skin had turned grey, like my own skin after I shifted and her fingers elongated, nails coming to a serrated tip. Her body shook as the shift finished. Only her arm had shifted. Black veins fanned out from her arm like the roots of a big willow tree. The dark lines stood out against her pale skin. Her eyes darkened and she smiled again at me, standing up straight.

"I am going to enjoy this." She spat out.

"What have you done?" I asked, taking two steps back. The creatures beside me growling and snarling.

Dr Springer laughed, "Dr Gelch has been doing some experiments, girl." He stood from behind the chair and walked over to Sophia. "Isn't she magnificent?"

"That is barbaric!" I yelled at him. "Sophia, why would you do this? Why would you want this life?"

She didn't answer and stepped towards me. Her eyes were almost too dark to see anymore.

"I wouldn't bother." Dr Springer laughed again. "She has lost all sense of self. She is a soldier for Dr Gelch, and therefore, she serves me too." He straightened his tie and stepped away from Sophia, putting distance between him and the inevitable fight coming.

Sophia curled her dangerous fingers and slashed through the air. Not aiming to strike me yet just showing off her new weapon.

"Sophia?" I yelled again, taking another step backwards.

The large creature stepped in front of me, shielding me from the threat. Sophia groaned and flung herself into the air. Dodging the large arm that tried to grab her. She rolled on the ground and charged again, her razor-like fingernails pointed directly for me.

I didn't have time to react. I put my arms up to brace for the fatal blow and closed my eyes. The sound of wet nails digging into flesh filled my ears, but when I opened my eyes. It was the smaller creature who was whimpering and gasping for air. He had stepped between me and Sophia and took the full brunt of her fatal blow.

"No!" I screamed, but it was too late.

Her long spindly fingers disappeared into the chest of the creature and she turned her arm slowly. The creature called out and scrambled to get out of her grasp. But she held him tighter, like she was clutching his heart in her hands. He looked over to me with tears welling in his eyes and gasped for his last breaths. She ripped her arm from his body and he fell to the floor limp. Black blood flowed from the huge cavity and spilled onto the white floor.

I ran to his side, crouching next to his dead body. I watched Sophia lick his blood off each of her fingers.

Black blood stained her lips.

I tried to put pressure on the gaping hole in his chest. But it was no use, I knew he was gone. Tears streamed down my face. He gave his life for me.

The larger creature roared in anger and attacked Sophia. She used all of her weight to push into Sophia and knocked her off her feet. The two of them threw blows at each other over and over. Spilling blood and snarling at each other with uncontrolled rage.

Then, the building shuddered, sending vibrations through the walls. I put my hands out to steady myself. The others did the same. It was enough to distract Sophia long enough that the creature grabbed her deformed arm in her mouth and ripped it clean off her body. Black and red blood spurted from the gaping wound. She coughed and spluttered and fell to the ground. Her human arm steadying her.

The creature wasted no time in ripping her head off next.

I couldn't help but to look away.

I turned to face Dr Springer, who was hiding behind the chair once again. Trembling and babbling nonsense to himself.

"Your turn." I said to him.

Then I turned to face my new friend.

*"Let's have some fun, shall we?"* I said to her through my mind and she bowed her head in agreement. *"Grab him. It's time he had a bath."* I said and the creature did as she was told.

She gripped him by the scruff of his lab coat and dragged him out the door. Dr Springer struggled to get free, but it was no use against the strength of my new friend. They followed me into the other room and I stood to the side as they passed me and moved further into the room. The damp air filled my lungs and my breath caught when I saw the tub again. Still filled with water.

"Have you ever tried your own machines, doctor?" I asked him, without looking in his direction.

"No, no, no! Please no! Don't" He pleaded as the creature dragged him closer to the tub. He dug his heels into the tiles as she effortlessly dragged him across the room. She threw him into the tub and I roughly placed the helmet on his head. I shoved the mask on his face and didn't bother with the mouthguard. He wouldn't need his teeth where he was going. I helped the creature push him under the water and clip the back of the helmet to the tub. She held his arms, while I firmly tethered his wrists to the sides of the tub. Making sure to slowly pull them tight, so they almost cut in. I leaned on the side of the tub and looked down at Dr Springer. Bubbles floating to the surface from his silent screams. When he stilled enough that I knew he could see me. I put my hand up in the air, three fingers outstretched and counted down.

Three... Two... One...

The machine rumbled to a start when I switched it on. I had no idea how to use the machine but decided to turn all the dials up to the highest setting. I stood back as it kicked into gear and roared loudly. I nodded to the creature to leave and followed her out.

With one last look back at the tub, which now had water thrashing over the sides of it, I smiled and closed the door behind me.

# Chapter 30

I stopped for a moment next to the small creature's body. Kneeling next to him, I folded his arms across his damaged chest and closed his eyes out of respect. I thanked him for his sacrifice and placed a gentle kiss on his forehead. I took Luke's bag from him and headed into the other hallway.

I found Luke in the hallway. He and the other large creature had dealt with Dr Gelch and looked triumphant. Luke stood there in his creature form, somehow bigger than I remembered him. The other creature stood to his left. Guarding his back fiercely. Luke's deep brown eyes met mine and he nodded in acknowledgment.

*"Let's get the hell out of here."* His voice shivered through my mind and I couldn't help but close my eyes to savour it.

"Where is Daniel?" I asked, remembering that he was somewhere down here too.

*"He told me he'd meet us up top. Let's go!"* Luke turned for the stairs we had taken and began his ascent.

I followed as fast as I could in my human form. Both creatures followed behind us. We ran, up and up, closer to freedom. Every breath felt like shards of glass in my lungs, but I did not stop. I knew there wasn't much longer until I could rest. Luke must have felt my exhaustion, because he turned to me and picked me up, swinging me onto his back. I held on tightly as he kept running, faster now that I wasn't trudging behind him.

*"Don't tell anyone I let you ride me."* He smirked up at me, and I laughed.

The first proper time I had laughed in a long time. I clutched his warm grey skin to mine and closed my eyes. He felt like home, like someone I had been waiting for my whole life.

Luke slowed and I sat up, sliding off his back once he'd stopped completely. The door in front of us had been welded shut. I stepped aside and Luke drew back his enormous arm, only needing one swing to knock the door off the wall. The evening breeze hit me first. Then I raised my nose to the sky and inhaled. I stepped through the threshold and took in the orange and purple sky. I stepped out into the open and inhaled the fresh air again. Letting it fill my lungs. Luke stepped out next and stood beside me, on edge and watching the distance. Then our two friends came out and stood either side of us. I smiled up at Luke as I realised that we had done it. We had escaped and could head home, to Illumina.

The shouts came first, then the gun shots.

Luke used his arm as a shield over me. The other two creatures surrounded us and roared, gnashing their teeth in the air. Whoever had ambushed us, had enough skill. They had attacked us at the entrance of the stairwell.

"*You either shift now or find cover!*" Luke's voice yelled through my head.

"I need to find Daniel." I yelled.

"*Shift or hide. Now!*" Luke commanded. And something inside me altered.

*My body began shifting without my consent. I had no choice. I didn't have time to take off Luke's clothes, but I dropped his bag to the ground just in time. My skin ripped through his black combat gear and it fell to the ground in ribbons.*

"How did you do that?" I growled at him. "How did you just make me shift?"

"Now is not the time." Luke turned from me. "I need you to fight like hell."

*I turned to face the attackers. I recognised the woman standing to the back. The same half shaved head and huge scar running over her face. The Snatchers who captured me weeks ago. My blood boiled as I stood next to Luke. The four of us could take them on. The Snatchers fired their weapons. We dodged them where we could, but most of the shots hit. We were too big to seek shelter, and too far away to strike. Thankfully, with our rapid healing, the shots wouldn't be enough to take us down. We edged closer, one of the other creatures finding a stray Snatcher, hiding behind an abandoned and rusted car. She lifted him into the air, the young man screamed as she ripped him apart. Throwing the remains in opposite directions. The Snatchers yelled commands at each other, falling back the closer we got.*

*Suddenly, the building blew up behind us. A huge explosion sending rubble from the lab flying across the sky.*

*Luke wrapped his arms around me and held me close. Even if I was in my creature form too, his need to protect me didn't change. The building shook as fire erupted from where it once stood. The ringing of the explosion sung through my head. Still vibrating the ground beneath us. I looked over to the Snatchers. The woman was laying on her side, confused by the explosion. I saw the opportunity before me and leapt from Luke's embrace. It took four bounds to reach her. With a swift motion, I pinned her down under my weight.*

*Growling low, saliva dripping from my lips. She cursed me and held onto my arms, as if she had a chance to move me from on top of her. Massive slabs of concrete fell beside me. But I did not move my gaze. She knew it was her end, although she didn't look scared. I pushed my weight down on her, squeezing any breath left out. She wheezed under me and spat at the ground where I stood. That was all I needed.*

*I wrapped my jaws around her head and ripped. Pulling harder than I needed to, to make sure I got the job done. Blood spurted from her neck, and I threw her head into the air. It fell in slow motion. Landing at the feet of the other two Snatchers watching. Their faces gaunt with fear. Trembling weapons in their hands.*

*They turned to run but were stopped in their tracks by the other two creatures who ripped them apart, limb from limb. Their screams echoed in my head as I returned to stand next to Luke. The building exploded again and fire erupted. It was then that I realised Daniel was nowhere to be seen. My eyes met Luke's and as if he read my mind, he wrapped his arms around me. Holding me in place and pulling me away from the flames and rubble. My heart dropped. I let out a desperate howl.*

*"Daniel!" I screamed through my mind. Luke held me tightly. He wouldn't let me go.*

*"Daniel!" I screamed again. Knowing he would not answer me.*

*"It's okay Melody." Luke said, calmly.*

*I slowly looked up at Luke, his dark eyes full of guilt.*

*"You knew?" I asked in disbelief. "You knew he wasn't going to make it out!" I punched my arm into his chest, but he held me. I screamed and screamed. A deafening roar broke from my throat as I slumped to the ground in agony.*

My body began shifting again as I took on my human form. Luke followed my lead and held onto me as we both shifted. The two creatures stood guard beside us. Luke shifted next to me and I sobbed in his arms until the sun dipped behind the smoke filled sky and night came. A shiver ran through me and goosebumps covered my exposed skin. Luke brushed his hand across my cheek and I opened my eyes.

"We need to get out of here, Melody." He said gently.

I nodded in response. I knew Daniel wouldn't want his sacrifice to be in vain. We still had to get to Illumina. Luke rummaged through his bag and pulled out spare clothes. I didn't have the energy to tease him about how many spare changes of clothes he packed. Instead I silently dressed and stood facing the wreckage. Luke came to stand beside me, placing his hand on the small of my back.

"The lab is gone." I said. "Won't they stop now?" I turned to face Luke.

"I don't think they will ever stop." He said, placing a gentle kiss on my forehead. "There will be many more just like Gelch and Springer. It's safer if we get to Illumina." Luke turned to pack up his bag and started walking towards the city.

I took one last look at the rubble and ruined building and swore to it in my head. The last few weeks had almost broken me. But I escaped. Daniel had saved us. Knowing he was not going to make it out. Tears welled in my eyes again and fell silently down my cheeks. I nodded to no one, in understanding of what Daniel had done. Then turned my back to the smouldering remains and followed Luke. Interlacing my fingers with his and holding him tight. The other two creatures followed closely behind.

~~~

It took us over an hour to make our way out of the dense part of the city. And with the dark night sky looming over us, we knew we needed to stop for rest. I knew I was heading into withdrawals, as my body became heavy and sluggish. A painful headache formed across my head, blurring my vision slightly.

I was grateful to hear Luke say, "This looks like a good place." Pointing to a small shop front.

It was mostly intact and just big enough to fit all four of us. But the creatures did not want to sleep in such close proximity and confined space. It had only one entrance, making it easy to guard. I found the wall with my outstretched hand to guide me and slumped to the ground. My body tremored slightly as I stilled. I hadn't spoken a word
~~~

since we left the wreck of the lab. I couldn't find the words. My mind thought only of Daniel and the other lives that were lost. Luke spoke to me in bits, keeping close but not expecting a response from me. I appreciated that.

"We need to find something to eat." Luke wasn't speaking to me, but to the huge creatures that lingered outside the little shop. They nodded and in unison, took off to hunt.

With my back leaned up against the wall, I brought my knees into my chest. Hugging them tightly and stared at my feet. Luke came to sit next to me and noticed the uncontrollable shivers that ran across my body.

"It's okay." He said, placing a solid hand on my knee, "Your body is withdrawing from the medication. It will ease soon. Your body heals quicker now." He wrapped his arm around me. I leant into the warmth of his body and rested my head on his chest. He took steady breaths and I began crying.

"Did he tell you anything?" I asked through sobs. My words were no more than a slur as the exhaustion overcame my body.

"He just made me promise to get you out." He tucked a stray hair behind my ear.

I felt like he was withholding information, but I was too tired to press any further. So instead, I let him hold me. I inhaled his scent and nuzzled my nose deeper into his chest. Luke gently held my chin with his thumb and finger, bringing my gaze up to his. He leaned in and kissed me gently. His lips were so soft against mine. When he pulled away to look at me again, a lone tear slid across his cheek. I let it fall onto my face and kissed him again.

The creatures had brought back an entire deer that was untouched by mutations. I was shocked and even went as far as to tease Luke about the one or two rabbits he had hunted when we were last in the forest. He nudged me flirtatiously and we laughed together. The four of us sat around a small fire Luke had made on the outside of the shop. The two creatures were still on guard, even though they must have been exhausted. I was able to create a makeshift bed for Luke and me to share. Using an old sheet I'd found in the corner of the room and Luke's bag as our pillow. We would sleep next to one another, for warmth and nothing more, I had told him. As the fire dimmed down to embers, we said good night to the creatures, who wanted to stay on the outside of the shop, guarding the entrance and we headed for the makeshift bed.

Sleep claimed me swiftly, even as the tremors worsened, exhaustion won.

# Chapter 31

Luke was up before the sun. Even though I felt like I could sleep for days, I followed him to the door of the shop. I knew we had a long journey ahead of us. The tremors had taken over my body, my hands unsteady as I reached out for him. My headache had lessened, and vision was normal again, thankfully.

"How long will it take us to get to Illumina?" I cleared my throat as I linked my arm through his.

He leaned casually on the door frame and welcomed me into his embrace. He managed to wear that same swagger he had the first day I met him. I snuggled close to his body and let him inhale my scent.

"One week, maybe less if we use our creature forms." His lips were drawn into a thin line. He noticed my tremors and held my hand steady. "How are you feeling?"

"As good as you would expect." I wasn't lying.

I knew he had been through the same withdrawals. Nausea rolled around my stomach and hot flushes came and went like the ocean tides. But I was alive and for that, I would be grateful.

He nodded silently. I didn't want to probe him for information on the last few days yet. I knew he would tell me what happened with Daniel when the time was right. The big male creature was on guard already, listening to the wind. Body tense and on alert. His chin was angled to the sky, to the last of the stars still scattered across the sky as it grew brighter with the morning. The female creature was lying on her side, just waking up and stretching her enormous body.

I looked around at the four of us, wondering how this strange group came to be. When only a few weeks ago, I was terrified to leave the comfort of my daily routine. The sun peaked in between the buildings, a bright orange. I put my shaking hand up to shield my eyes and squinted as I looked at the sun. The morning promised a new beginning, a new future for me and for Luke. But there was a pain in my heart at the thought that Daniel wouldn't be a part of that future.

We packed up our belongings and headed for the edge of the city. The large creatures kept close enough, sometimes wandering off. But never too far. We kept our pace as quick and quiet as we could. I needed to stop more often than wanted as the withdrawal symptoms ebbed and flowed. We had no idea if there were people looking for us. Or if any of the Snatchers had got away and alerted other groups.

"Do you think we could help them shift back to their human forms?" I pointed to the two creatures walking with us.

"I have had the same thought." Luke mused, rubbing his chin gently. "I don't know if they have been shifted for too long. Or if their deformities from the experiments will make it impossible."

"Maybe someone in Illumina can help." I said hopeful.

Luke nodded but his face told me that he wasn't sure.

We kept heading for the edge of the city. The buildings had decayed even more since the last time I remembered walking these streets. Only skeletons remained of what was once a thriving city, stood their ground. Vines and grass overgrown and reclaiming the terrain. Wet newspapers scattered the ground. And the humid air filled my lungs, making it hard to breathe. We walked all day, sometimes not speaking for hours. I emptied the contents of my stomach when I couldn't push the nausea back down. My thoughts were on Daniel while we walked the streets. Everything he sacrificed for our freedom. I wasn't sure what Luke was thinking about, but he glanced over to me a few times, guilt and grief plastered on his face. Maybe I didn't want to know what he knew. Maybe it was better to not know. I wouldn't ask him until he was ready and maybe he would never bring it up.

The air was cooling and the sun was dipping behind the buildings. We had reached the outskirts of the city. The neighbourhoods of homes and playgrounds that I had grown up on. Nausea churned in the depths of my stomach and I wasn't sure if it was the withdrawals or memories these streets held.

"It'll take another hour to reach the forest." Luke said, pointing ahead of us. The creatures nodded in understanding and the big male took off ahead. To make sure it was safe. "Do you want to stop here for the night, or keep on going until we reach the forest?" Luke turned to face me.

"I don't want to stay here." I replied. Exhaustion lacing each word. My skin was clammy and wan. "Will the Snatchers still be after us?"

"There might be more Snatchers after us. I have no idea how many are in a group. Or how many groups there are." Luke spoke cautiously. As if he was calculating how many we had killed.

"I want to get as far away from the city, the lab and the Snatchers as we possibly can."

"I know, but you're exhausted." He placed his arms either side of me. Holding my hips. He placed the back of his hand on my forehead. "You're burning up." Drawing his eyebrows together, he pulled me closer to him and kissed me where his hand had been. I was exhausted, but I did not want to be caught again.

"Let's just keep going." I reassured him. He nodded and we picked up the pace. We walked quickly through the neighbourhood. The creatures had disappeared, keeping to the darkest shadows. My eyes darted around, trying to sense any movement or danger. When I spotted the street sign of my home address, I stilled. It hadn't crossed my mind that we were so close to my old house. The house where I grew up with Daniel, my mother and father. So many memories. The house where my mother betrayed us and handed us over to the Snatchers. I vomited.

"Come on Melody." Luke gently rubbed my back and held my hand tightly to tug me along.

I stared back at the street sign as we headed down another street. I couldn't shake that same feeling of betrayal. I wondered what happened to my mother after we escaped.

A feral growl sounded and Luke stilled. He held his arms out to shield me as I came up behind him. Standing behind his broad shoulders. We listened as the growling and snarling got more intense. We backed up against a tall fence and Luke peered around the corner. I watched the back of his head for any sign of reaction, but he was still and unmoving. He turned to face me and used his index finger to tell me to be quiet. I gave him a look that suggested I already knew that. Then he pointed across the road and signalled with his hand for me to follow him. We ran across the road to the fence on the other side. I crouched down low and made sure to stay in the shadow that the fence cast out. We crept silently across the streets, each movement calculated and fast. The growls were getting further away with each street that we passed. The two other creatures we had befriended were nowhere to be seen. As night fell, we came to the last street. I could see the grassy edge of the forest and the looming trees ahead. We were both eager to get into the cover of the trees and our steps quickened until we were running. Faster and faster, holding my breath until I felt the soft earth beneath my feet. I didn't look back at the city as we sprinted into the forest.

Luke was right beside me, running. We ran until we couldn't run anymore. Until the city was but a shadow in the night sky. We stopped at the base of a giant tree and caught our breath. The forest air was fresh and smelt like the dirt was damp from a recent storm. The ground felt soft under my shoes and I stretched my arms up above my head at the almost instant relief I felt being away from the city.

"Don't get too comfortable yet." Luke laughed. "We still need to make it through the forest."

I laughed and he nudged me before bringing me in close and holding me tightly.

"Thank you for rescuing me." I whispered into his chest. And he squeezed me tighter.

We found a tree for the night and I climbed up. My tremors had thankfully eased, but the nausea came with a vengeance. My skin was still sickly and I knew Luke was keeping a close eye on me. The other two creatures still hadn't shown up, but I was sure they wouldn't be too far behind. They would be able to handle themselves in the forest, so I wasn't worried. Once we found a sturdy branch, Luke leaned his back against the tree trunk and I sat in between his legs with my back to his chest. He wrapped his strong arms around my body and I let out a long exhale. I had never felt so at home with a person before.

"I don't remember my life before you Melody." Luke whispered into my ear. My eyes were closed as I listened to his breathing. The beating of his heart pulsed under my head and I felt my own heartbeat skip to match the rhythm of his.

"I don't want to remember my life before you." I whispered back. Angling my head towards his.

The moon light shone upon his face, casting shadows over his eyes and lips. I lifted my chin and he leant down and kissed me. His mouth parted and I felt the unspoken hunger in his wordless motion. My hand came up to his neck and I pulled him closer, wanting more. Our souls became one and we slept in each other's embrace all night. It was the best sleep I've had in years.

# Chapter 32

The sun warmed my face as it rose in the morning sky. The fog over my mind had lifted, a brand-new day promised. Luke's arms were still tightly wrapped around me as he slept. I looked up at him and watched his beautiful face. Usually he wore a tense expression, his brow was often drawn to a frown and his lips a thin line. But while he slept, he looked peaceful. Like his mind was quiet and his features were able to soften. I moved on the branch to turn and face him and brushed my fingers across his forehead, moving a tight curl from his face. He stirred awake at my touch and smiled when he saw me staring.

"Good morning sunshine." He said through his raspy morning voice. "You have colour in your cheeks again."

I smiled and leant in to kiss him on his cheek, then started my descent to the forest floor. Tremors passed through my body sporadically and I hoped I was through the worst of it. My stomach rumbled to remind me that we hadn't eaten all day yesterday and though the nausea was holding on tightly, I knew I needed to eat.

"I am starving." I said when I reached the forest floor and looked back up the tree to find Luke climbing down right behind me. He was so agile and made it look effortless.

"You read my mind." He patted his stomach and stretched his body. "You know what would be really fun?" He lifted his eyebrows at me, with a menacing expression across his face.

"What?" I laughed, not knowing what he was about to say.

"If we went hunting in our creature forms." He looked at me with a predatory smile.

I smiled back at him, "That does sound fun. Doesn't it?" I replied and began removing my clothes slowly.

Luke watched me as I dropped each item of clothing to the ground. Walking around the tree as I did. He followed me, removing his clothes too. Until we both stood next to each other, naked. He held out his hand for me to hold and I did so without breaking his stare. Then we took deep breaths and started to shift.

*I stood up on my strong legs, inhaling the scents of the forest. All withdrawal symptoms I suffered before had vanished, as though my creature form overpowered them. I could smell each leaf, each tree and all the rocks and grasses surrounding us. Luke watched me as I fell back down to all fours and felt the earth beneath my feet and hands. I dug my nails in deep and rolled my head around once. Stretching out my new body.*

*"Ready?" Luke's voice swept through my mind and I nodded.*

*We took off running. I could hear the flapping of bird wings, coming from miles away. The wind blew through the trees, whispering to the leaves and carrying scents through the forest. Footsteps sounded up ahead. Four legs, not two. Light steps, and crunching sounds. Likely a deer eating. I sniffed the air and caught her scent. Luke had smelt her too. We slowed our running and made our steps lighter as we neared the deer. She was grazing in an opening and looked to be alone.*

*Luke looked over at me and grinned. His jagged teeth were wet with saliva and his breathing was heavy. His dark brown eyes were the only fragments of his human form, yet I still thought he was beautiful.*

*I nodded to him to make the kill and he lunged forward. The deer didn't have any time to react as Luke's mouth gripped her throat and she was dead within a second. A quick and painless death. She didn't deserve to suffer. We just needed to eat. Luke held the deer in his jaws as he walked back towards me. Blood dripped from the wound on her neck and the smell of sweet iron filled my nostrils. I felt my pupils dilate as he dropped the kill at my feet.*

*"A special breakfast for you." Luke said and bowed low, not breaking my gaze. I bowed my head at him dramatically and then began eating my meal. Luke joined in and we finished off the meat within moments. When we had finished licking every bone, we headed back towards the tree where we had left our clothes.*

*"You have to admit." Luke said into my mind. "This shifting thing can be quite fun."*

*"When it's controlled. I suppose." I said back. Though it took more effort than I remembered.*

We stopped at the tree and I began shifting back, my bones and skin cracking and popping back into place. Nausea swept over my body again, although dulled as my stomach willed the food to stay down. I held the back of my neck while I rolled it from side to side. It was always harder for me to get used to shifting back to my human form, my body felt so foreign.

"I will never get used to that." I said to Luke who was standing behind me while I dressed. He was still in his creature form, I realised. When I finished buttoning my pants up, I turned to face him. He was guarding me, body tense and his nose up in the air, sniffing intensely.

"What is it?" I asked, walking up beside him. He used his long, muscled arm to push me behind him. Being careful not to injure me with his sharp nails. I searched the forest floor with my eyes, but I couldn't see anything. Luke's heightened senses in his creature form picked up something my human senses couldn't.

"*Stay behind me.*" He commanded me and I obeyed.

I heard footsteps creeping towards us. Not trying to be silent but carefully stepping as if they were stalking towards us. I stayed behind Luke, who had now backed me up against the tree, so I was covered from all angles.

"Luke?" I whispered. "What is wrong?"

A low growl came from his throat and I knew it was a warning growl. I peeked around his body and saw multiple figures heading towards us. I recognised the large male creature as they neared. He was the large creature we had escaped the lab with. As they came closer into view, I noticed that he had a muzzle strapped to his face and his arms were bound tightly together. There were five Snatchers with him. One of them held onto a leash that was wrapped around the creature's wrists and tugged roughly forcing the creature to keep walking. Luke growled again and I could tell that he was sizing up the competition. The other Snatchers were armed with a variety of weapons. Two of them stood closely behind the creature. Holding long, thin weapons with a taser on the tip. Both pressing it into the creature's back and zapping him to keep moving. The creature stiffened and growled every time the taser met his skin, but he did not struggle. The other two Snatchers were just as armed and alert as they stalked closer.

"Well, well, well. Look what we have here fellas." The lead Snatcher said as he forcefully pulled the lead again and the creature fell to his knuckles on the ground. His skin was covered in bruises and wounds that looked old and new. The sounds we had heard last night in the neighbourhood must have been him and the other female creature fighting against the Snatchers. They had captured them last night and beaten him so badly. A whimper left my lips as I realised that we had abandoned them.

"Looks like we found ourselves another toy, Boss." One of the Snatchers in the back replied. He was a skinny man. Gaunt features and missing teeth.

Luke growled more intensely and the Snatcher laughed in response. They pointed their weapons at Luke and edged closer again. I stumbled on a tree root that was sticking up out of the ground and caught the attention of one of the Snatchers.

"Hold on a minute." He pointed right at me. "Is that a human girl?" The others looked to where he was pointing, directly at me. Luke stepped in front of me and made himself bigger to shield me. "Looks like we interrupted this creature enjoying a meal." They all laughed again, a filthy, taunting laugh that only promised violence.

"Actually, no." I said, picking up Luke's sword and fought against my nausea to straighten up. I stepped out from behind Luke and walked out to stand beside him. "We have already eaten. But we don't mind having some fun." I pointed the heavy sword towards them. An invitation to fight.

*"Are you sure about this Melody?"* Luke asked. Planting his feet solidly into the earth.

I nodded towards him and smirked at the Snatchers who were staring dumbstruck at what they were seeing. I was almost sure they had never seen a woman fight alongside a creature before.

*"Where is the other creature?"* Luke asked our captive friend. He bowed his head lower and grunted deeply, shaking his head. My heart dropped in my chest.

She didn't make it. They had killed her.

Luke lunged forwards and slashed his arms through the air, the Snatchers retaliating with their weapons. The tasers ripped into Luke's skin, and he winced away in pain. Blood trickled from his shoulder, where the weapon had zapped him. I looked closer at the weapon. They had reinforced it with a blade. One small knife-like blade, strapped to the side of it like a spear. Not only were they tasering their *toys*, as they called us, but they were stabbing them shallowly each time too.

"Hurts, doesn't it?" The lead Snatcher laughed. "We had these bad boys reinforced with poison blades." He stroked his deadly spear with such gentleness. Truly admiring it.

"You're going to regret this." I spat out at him, baring my teeth.

"How did you get to run with these monsters, girl?" His voice was low, a genuine question.

I didn't reply and we stalked around in a circle. The creature and two of the other Snatchers kept to the sideline. They stabbed and tasered him over and over. His body weakened with every little blow. I could see his eye becoming dull with whatever poison was laced on the blades.

*"Luke, we need to get this over and done with."* I shot through my mind.

*"That poison is strong. I can feel it eating away at me already."* Luke's voice wavered as he stumbled next to me.

The creature groaned and I turned to look at him. Fading away, he angled with his head for us to run, to leave him and get away.

"I won't leave you." I said towards the creature.

"Stupid girl!" One of the Snatchers spat on the ground at his feet. "They're just dumb creatures. Not worth a pretty thing like you dying over." He looked me over with his roaming eyes and winked at me.

Something territorial in Luke snapped and threw himself through the air. The Snatcher didn't have time to react as

Luke tore him apart. Blood and gore lacing the forest floor around them. Luke staggered as he rose to his feet daring the others to step forward.

*"I didn't like his tone."* He wiped the man's blood off his chin and glared at the lead Snatcher. Who was stone faced as he stumbled backwards.

"How are you controlling them?" He yelled at me.

"I'm not." I replied, not a lie.

Luke stood tall on all four legs as he came to stand beside me. The forest seemed to stop around us. Silently watching as we stood our ground. The wind whispered as it blew strands of my hair out of my braid and across my face. I looked at the Snatchers through my brows and took a step forward. One of the Snatchers who had kept to the back raced forwards and Luke lunged towards him. Ripping his head clean off his shoulders. The body dropped to the floor limp and my eyes met the remaining three Snatchers. They raced towards us, weapons at the ready. I ran towards the thin man, Luke at my side. I knew Luke would want to take on the lead Snatcher and I had no desire to fight him myself. I held Luke's sword above my head and brought it down swiftly. It connected with the Snatchers taser and I knocked it down. I held his weapon to the ground with my own and threw a punch which landed right on his jaw. Pain shot through my knuckles, and I drew back shaking my hand. The scrawny man laughed and spat blood onto the ground. He turned to smile up at me. His bloody gums glistened in the morning light.

"Now how'd a pretty little thing like you learn to fight?" He taunted.

"I had a good teacher." Was all I replied before I swung the sword at him again. He swerved out of the way this time and hurled his own fist towards me. The impact of his fist in my guts was enough to wind me. I stumbled back and tried to catch my breath. My weapon fell from my hands as I grasped my stomach, trying to get air into my lungs.

Luke and the lead Snatcher were brawling. Luke was still just as agile as I remember him being. A lethal weapon, with army training. His creature form was no different. Manoeuvring his body to avoid the attacks from the weapon being jabbed at him. Luckily the Snatcher fought with such rage, that it blurred his ability to stay calm. Something I remember Luke telling me when he trained us. Keep calm. Luke swung his enormous arm and it struck the lead Snatcher, knocking him to the ground.

I tried to steady my breathing as I stumbled to the ground. The slender Snatcher stood above me, holding Luke sword to my throat. He cleared his throat and whistled to get Luke's attention. Luke stilled immediately, growling deeply.

"That's right, creature." The man above me said cruelly. "Unless you want me to kill your precious human friend, I'd suggest you step away. Now!" He dug the tip of the sword into my neck and I felt the warm sensation of blood gliding down my skin. I didn't dare take my eyes off the man.

# Chapter 33

Luke surrendered.

He ignored my demands to kill every last one of them and rescue the captive creature. He ignored the profanities I sent through my mind to him when he let the men tie up his arms and shoved him to his knees. The slender Snatcher grabbed my arms and pulled me up to my knees so I could watch as the other two brutally stabbed both of the creatures in front of me. Luke winced with every blow. His head was hanging low.

I screamed each time he was struck, as I watched the life being torn from both Luke and the other creature, the latter now laying on his side. Gulping for air to enter his lungs. The Snatchers laughed, mocking me. Tears streamed down my face. My eyes did not risk looking away from Luke. In case that was his last breath.

"What makes these creatures so special?" The man whispered into my ear. His breath stunk of rotten teeth and his last meal. "Why die for them?" He laughed again, standing up straight.

His fingers twisted through my braid as I knelt in front of him. I held my hands over the top of his, making sure he didn't rip my hair right off my scalp. He held Luke's sword in his other hand, ready to strike me at any moment.

I whispered under my breath, barely loud enough for the Snatcher to hear.

"What? Speak up girlie!" He leaned down close to my face again. Pulling my hair back so I had to look at him.

"*Melody, don't!*" Luke yelled at me.

"I said," I started, smiling up at him. "Because I *am* one of them." My smile grew.

He scrunched his nose up in confusion. I let my hands go from his, which was still entwined in my braid, holding me firmly.

*I smiled wider as my skin started to bubble, my arms snapped back and forth. The bones in my body contorted and Luke's clothes ripped off my body. The pale tone of my skin changed to the beautiful dark grey I had come to love.*

"What the..." *The man stumbled back and fell to the ground on his behind. Crawling away along the forest floor as I stood up. With their eyes wide and mouths open, they gawked up at me. Now in my full creature form. Weapons drawn and frozen with shock. They watched.*

*My throat rumbled and I thrust myself towards the man on the ground. He couldn't avoid my wrath as I tore him open. His insides poured out, staining the beautiful moss and grass beneath him. I turned to face the other two Snatchers. They both stammered their words, as they tried to make sense of what had just happened. Luke used the last of his strength to lean into the lead Snatcher and knock him off his feet. The other Snatcher stabbed the creature lying down over and over, trying to end his life quicker.*

*Footsteps sounded behind me and before I could see what was coming, a small object flew across my vision. Landing between me and the others. When it impacted on the ground, the device spewed a dense smoke. Obstructing my view of them. I tried to move forward through the smoke, but my heightened smell and senses couldn't tolerate it. I coughed and spluttered as I grasped my throat. I could hear the others coughing too, it had affected them in the same way.*

*With stealth, I saw someone moving through the smoke. Nothing more than a dark shadow. Slashing and stabbing as they went. I heard the sound of thuds as bodies hit the floor and anger raged through me. I snarled and tried to move forward again. I had to get to Luke. I was met with the same stinging in my throat. I couldn't breathe. My body started to shift back to my human form, more painful than I remembered. I screamed and gasped for air before I lost consciousness.*

<div align="center">~~~</div>

I groaned, turning over. Flinching at every sore muscle in my body. I heard unfamiliar voices around me. I tried to open my eyes, but my eyelids were too heavy. My head throbbed. I sat up and tried again to open my eyes, squinting at first. My vision was blurry, even blinking didn't clear them. I held my head to try to steady my dizziness.

"Take it easy." Said a male voice near me.

I looked around the room. Not room, tent. It was a small brown tent. Large enough only for the bed I was lying on, and a table on the opposite side. A figure stood beside the bed, hands outstretched towards me, as if I were about to fall.

"W-what…" I started but choked on my dry throat. I winced with every cough as my abdominal muscles tense and cramped under the movement.

"Hold on. Take it easy." The voice came again. Then a glass of water was placed into my hands. "Drink this, it'll help with your throat." I sipped on the water and wiped away the tears that had welled in my eyes from coughing. I blinked my eyes rapidly, trying again to unblur my vision. But it was no use.

"Your vision should return to normal within an hour or so. It's from the smoke bomb." The man spoke softly.

"Who are you?" I managed to say with a hoarse voice.

"My name is Jax. I am with the rebel group." He sat on the side of my bed and gently ushered me to sip the water again.

"Rebel group?" I repeated, in question. "Where am I?" I asked, blinking hard.

"Some of our scouts found you and some others in a bit of trouble with the Snatchers. So, they got you out and brought you here. This is one of our camps." He laughed.

I shook my head trying to make sense of what he said. But my headache had become more painful and throbbed hard into my temples. I sucked on my teeth through my lips and held my eyes shut with my fingers.

"Lay down, rest some more. You'll feel better this afternoon." Jax said, helping me to lay down again.

"The others," I said, without opening my eyes. "The others I was with, are they okay?"

Jax held my hand and squeezed it tightly. "They're fine. Rest up and we will talk more when you feel better."

I let the darkness consume me. Let the weightlessness of dreaming take me far away. Somewhere where my family hadn't been torn apart, where I had lived a normal life. Where I met Luke the normal way and still fell in love with him. My body sank into the thin, lumpy mattress below me and I let it swallow me whole.

~~~

When I awoke again, Jax was right, I felt much more clear in my head. Although my body still ached. I sat up and blinked my eyes into focus, able to take in the room properly. The bed was barely a bed, a fold out stretcher bed with a very uncomfortable mattress. The table on the opposite side had small jars and a mixing bowl on top. They looked like medicines and herbs of some sort. I swung my legs over the side of the bed. My stomach felt a little queasy, so I sat for a moment before trying to stand. I looked down at the new clothes I was wearing. I had shifted while wearing Luke's combat clothes, so they were torn to shreds. I wore brown linen pants and a dark green linen top. Not very flattering, but they were comfortable at least. Listening to the noises on the outside of the tent, I could hear people talking to one another, walking, fire crackling and the sound of metal banging too. I couldn't hear any voices I knew.
~~~

A *rebel group*, Jax had said this was. I stood up from the bed and felt surprisingly fine. I found a piece of black leather to tie around my waist, to give me some sort of shape. Then I made my way out the opening of the tent. I stepped out into the middle of a campsite. The rebel group was much larger than I had expected. Tents erected every five or so meters from the next. They ran in two rows, each tent opposite another with little campfires between them. There were more people than I had seen in a very long time. Everyone was wearing the same green and brown shades of linen clothing, and everyone was busy. Busy with some sort of job they no doubt had earned to become a part of this group.

"Hey, Melody!" Jax shouted. "Over here." He waved his arm in the air like a proud parent at a school play. He was smiling from ear to ear while he half jogged over to me.

His shoulder length hair was woven into thin dreadlocks, and it bounced with every step he took. The roots were dark brown and the ends looked like they had been dipped in sunlight. His dark chocolate skin contrasted against the green of his linen shirt. And his deep smile lines gave me the impression that he wore that smile often. I met his eyes, and they caught me off guard, one of them a light golden brown and the other was splashed with the lightest blue. He stopped at an arms reach from me.

"Glad you're feeling better." He said.

"Thank you." I replied flatly. "Where are the others you found me with?" I asked.

I had planned to wait until they offered to take me, but I was too impatient for that.

"Yes, the others." He scratched his soft chin. He must have been a few years younger than me. "Well the man with curly dark hair…"

"Luke." I said a little too abruptly.

"Ah, sure, Luke. He hasn't woken up yet. But he is fine." He put both hands up in front of him defensively when he caught my glare. "He needed an antidote for the poison, but he was very upset when you were taken away. So the healers needed to sedate him."

I nodded. "Take me to him."

"He needs to rest. He won't know you're there anyway and besides, there's some…"

"Take me to him." I repeated without breaking my stare.

Jax nodded quickly and pointed to another tent a few metres away. "Okay, but we can't stay long. The healers get snappy if we linger."

We walked over to the tent and I ducked my head to get through the door. There were six separate fold out beds lined up. Three on either side of the spacious room. Only four of the beds were occupied. Two wounded rebels, one elderly man and on the furthest bed was Luke. My heart stopped in my chest for a moment and I gasped. The two healers stopped to glance our way and then returned to their work. Luke's curly black hair and pale face lay peacefully on the stretcher bed. He looked so much smaller in here. His clothes were the same green and brown linen as mine and the others and there was a fluid line in his arm, hooked to the tent roof above him. I walked quickly to his bedside and knelt down next to him.

"Oh Luke." I whispered, grabbing his hand in mine and kissing it softly.

"*Luke.*" I sent through my mind to him. But he did not flinch.

A tear escaped my eye and I wiped my cheek before anyone noticed.

"What is in this?" I said pointing to the fluid line. Jax shrugged and the healers didn't indulge me. "Excuse me, when will he be conscious?" I asked one of the healers directly.

"A day, maybe more." She said quietly.

"Will he be okay?"

"Shh." The other healer spat out at me. "These patients need rest." One of the wounded rebels groaned and rolled over on the bed.

"I need to be made aware as soon as he is awake." I demanded, keeping my voice as low as I could. "Where is the other creature I was with?"

The healer gave Jax a pointed look.

"Yeah, we should go." Jax held my shoulders and pulled me to my feet. I shrugged him off me and grabbed Luke's hand again, kissing it once more. Jax placed a hand on my back and nudged me towards the door.
"Keep moving, please." He whispered so only I could hear.

"Where is the other creature I was with?" I asked as soon as we left the tent.

Jax held my arm and led me away, out of earshot of the healers.

"He is alive. But he needed more treatment. More than what the healers could do here." He said.

"What does that mean?" I spat out.

"The creature had a lot of poison in his body. He couldn't even shift back. So, we transported the creature back to base." He started to walk off but turned to face me, smiling broadly. "I have someone who is really keen to see you."

We left the healers tent and walked through the path between the tents. Everyone was in good spirits. Some people were sparring in a makeshift ring on the outside of the tent rows. Their swords clanking on one another loudly and powerfully. I took in the surroundings and watched the people as they scurried about. Jax stopped in front of a tent and turned to face me. The tent was as unremarkable as the rest. Jax's smile took over his face. His teeth were not straight, but they were the whitest I had seen. His smile was enough to brighten anyone's day. I raised my eyebrow at him in confusion and followed him into the tent.

# Chapter 34

I walked into the tent, ducking to get through the door and looked around the room. It was the same as the room I had woken up in. A small table, covered in little nick-nacks and a fold out bed. Jax cleared his throat and the figure sitting on the bed turned to face us. My whole body froze. My heart stopped beating for a moment. My knees were weak and a lump formed in my throat.

"Hey Mel. Thought you'd finally wake up?" He said laughing. His smile, his beautiful smile. He ran a hand through his dirty blonde hair and stood up to greet me. His hazel eyes met mine and a small noise escaped my throat. Tears spilled down my cheeks silently and I realised I hadn't taken a breath.

"Not going to give your brother a hug?" Daniel outstretched his arms and I practically fell into them. I took a sharp breath in and then everything came pouring out of me. I cried and Daniel pat me on the back firmly.

"I guess you missed me then." He laughed, pulling away.

"I thought you were dead!" I yelled, punching him in the arm. I wiped my tears away and laughed with Daniel. Jax stood near the doorway and awkwardly laughed too. I turned to face him.

"Why wasn't this the first thing you told me?" I snapped at him.

"Well, I did try. But you were concerned about Luke." He shrugged nervously.

"Don't worry about my big sister Jax. She doesn't like surprises. Or anything else really." He teased and nudged Jax hard on the back. "Thanks, you can leave us now." Jax smiled and went to walk out of the tent.

"Wait." I said, and Jax turned to face me, "Thank you." I smiled and Jax nodded before leaving. I turned to face Daniel again and looked him over. I was in disbelief. Only moments ago, he was dead, then suddenly, here he is. Alive and well. Thriving apparently.

"Okay, so should you start or should I?" Daniel mused.

"You. Tell me everything." I sat down on the small wooden stool that was tucked under the table.

Which Daniel had turned into his workbench. I wasn't surprised at all. He smiled and gave me a *well what did you expect* look before beginning his explanation.

He told me about how he and Luke planned to rescue me. That they were going to break into the lab and that he had some sort of relationship with Dr Gelch that allowed them to sneak in. He brushed over that information, and

I mentally noted to ask him about that later. They decided to separate to cover more ground quickly; Daniel was to set the explosions and Luke was to find me. After he had set the first lot of explosives, he met a nurse named Janice on the way to the lowest level to plant the bomb. My heart pounded in my chest as he told his story. My throat caught at the mention of the old nurse's name. But I stayed silent as he continued to tell me about the cells on the lowest level. Who he found there and that Janice and Greg Osbourn sacrificed themselves to save everyone.

"After I left Janice and Greg, I went into the tunnels with the patients she had gotten out. I closed the huge iron door and sealed it. Then we ran, as fast as we could. It was pitch black, except for my little torch. When the bomb went off, we were still in the tunnel. It was pretty hectic for a while there. The tunnel half collapsed and we had rubble falling on us. A lot of the patients didn't make it. Some of them were crushed in the explosion and some were too weak to make it out of the tunnels. But I got a handful of them out and into the city. Then we made a run for the forest. I couldn't risk meeting you and Luke where we agreed, but I knew he would bring you into the forest. So we waited. That's when I bumped into these guys." Daniel pointed to the tent around us. "I basically stumbled on their camp site and they were all in a panic. They had heard the explosion and were going crazy. Didn't know which rebel group pulled it off." He laughed.

"What do you mean *which rebel group*?" I asked.

"There is a whole army of rebels. They're grouped off into smaller troops. I think there has got to be about five more." He nodded in amusement. "And apparently, they have been trying to infiltrate the lab for a very long time. And *we* pulled it off." He said proudly.

I stared at the ground. Taking in everything he had just told me. There were other rebel groups, many more. And we had destroyed the lab.

"Are you going to say anything?" Daniel said flatly. I stuttered and when I couldn't find the words, he said, "Your turn then." The smile vanished from his face.

I told him everything that had happened from the moment I was taken by the Snatchers, until I had woken up on this day. He listened intensely, putting all the pieces together. Merging our stories until they made sense.

"Okay." He finally said, scratching his chin. "So, Dr Gelch was making an army, an army of creatures. That he controlled?"

I nodded.

"But we destroyed the lab. So surely, they can't do that again." He wasn't really asking a question.

"Luke said the army will be after us now more than ever. We may have destroyed the lab, but the army is still out there. The Snatchers are still out there. It's just a matter of time before another lab is created and they start all over again. They might even have multiple labs across the city."

We sat in silence, only asking some questions here and there about each other's past few weeks. Then shouting sounded from outside the tent. Daniel shot up to his feet and ran out quickly. I followed and when I stepped out of the tent, night had fallen. The only light was coming from the campfires scattered between the tents. We had been talking for hours. My stomach grumbled and I placed my hand across my body. I couldn't remember the last time I had eaten a proper meal. I stood next to Daniel and looked in the directions of everyone's attention.

"What's happening?" I whispered to Daniel.

"The scouting team is back, with their leader." He pointed towards the commotion and a small group of rebels, who were jogging into the camp.

Some were head to toe in black fighting leathers and the others wore the same green and brown linen clothing. All the scouting team were armed to the teeth with weapons and protective gear. They wore padding across their arms and thighs. With large metal plates protecting their chests and shoulders. Weapons swung across their bodies and in their hands. Guns, swords, daggers. You name it. The crowd was murmuring loudly when they approached. They parted and allowed the scouting team to reach the centre. They stood in the middle of the rebel group. Others were at their sides immediately, taking their weapons, giving them water and relieving them of the heavy protection they wore.

Through the middle of the crowd, a tall gentleman walked through. His eyes were locked on Daniel as he strode across the camp. He had to be in his late fifties. With white hair and a well-groomed beard to match. His icy hair was tied back neatly into a ponytail and his white beard was groomed into a point that hung to where his neck met his chest. He walked with confidence and wore a black uniform. It hugged his broad shoulders and outlined every detail of his muscles. Showing that he was a force to be reckoned with. As he got closer to Daniel and me, I noticed he wore a pendant around his neck. The same as Luke's, only the silver detailing on the outside was slightly different. He cleared his throat and stopped a mere inch from Daniel's face.

"Your weapons, Daniel." His voice bellowed across the camp as everyone watched the interaction. "They were marvellous!" He shouted and the rebel camp cheered with a victorious roar that shook the ground.

Daniel smiled, shaking the broad leader's hand and then pushed me forwards, the attention of the ruggedly handsome rebel now on me.

"This is my sister, Melody. The one I was telling you about."

The gentleman studied me, frowning. "I see." He extended his hand. I nervously shook it, his firm grip almost making me yelp.

"Nice to finally meet you, Melody. Your brother has told me a lot about you." He leaned in closer, not loosening his grip on my hand.

"I will need you to fill me in on everything, once you're feeling up to it of course." Then he released my hand and walked away. The crowd followed him and the rest of the scouting team down the campsite and into one of the larger tents.

"Who was that?" I asked. Rubbing my palm and flexing my fingers from the pain that still lingered there.

"That's the leader of this rebel group. Tobias." He said.

"As in, *the* Tobias? From Luke's stories of Illumina?" I gasped.

"The very same." He smiled. Then he began to walk towards the now bustling tent, filled with laughter and chatter.

"Wait! Do you mean..." I chased after him.

"These rebel groups have come from Illumina." He grinned and walked off into the brightness of the tent.

I gazed at the starry night for a moment longer, before following him into the tent.

A band with fiddles and drums sat in the far corner of the tent, an upbeat tune playing. The music was loud and the atmosphere was cheerful. Daniel and I sat on a small table on the border of the big tent. This tent, I had learned, was the common gathering area. Where the rebels shared their meals, where they celebrated and where they mourned. It was larger than the other tents, with many tables and chairs scattered across the floor. There was a buffet table at the head of the tent, covered with an array of different foods. There was flatbread, meat cooked in herbs, roasted vegetables and some desserts. I wondered how they got all the food here. But Daniel explained that they made most of it on the road, the cooks were very knowledgeable and could live off the land. Some of the ingredients they brought from Illumina. Everyone had a meaningful job here, whether they were on the scouting team, fighters, teachers, healers, cooks, or something else. Everyone had a place, a purpose. I was beginning to feel the warmth of the tent. The joy everyone felt, even if they had no idea what tomorrow would bring.

Tobias and his scouting team sat at a large table, laughing and discussing what they found on their outing. Sometimes whispering low to keep the information private. Tobias' eyes caught me staring from across the room and he raised his glass to me. I nodded my head, out of respect, and looked towards the other groups of people enjoying themselves. Daniel was bobbing along to the music and enjoying himself, he didn't notice when I slipped away to go visit Luke.

I walked through the passage between the tents, taking in the silence of the night, except for the humming of the music. The stars were bright in the sky. I hadn't ever noticed them in the city. The little campfires cracked and hissed as I walked past them. When I reached the healers tent, I paused at the entrance, listening. One of the healers was humming a beautiful tune. One I had heard before. I tried to remember where I had heard it. I slowly stepped into the tent and greeted the healer with a slight nod of my head. She returned the greeting but did not waver her humming. I walked across the tent and to Luke's side. He hadn't moved since the last time I saw him. I sat on a stool next to his bed and held his hand tightly in mine. Watching his chest rise and fall under the light blanket. Colour had come back to his face and his eye sockets didn't look so dull now. I was grateful to see the improvement, even if it was only slight. I listened to the tune the healer hummed and closed my eyes. I swayed side to side as the song seeped into my body. My ears heard it, but my body absorbed it and became it. I felt it working its way through my veins, enveloping any feelings I had. Making me numb. The song was all I could hear, could feel. The ground beneath me pulsed as the humming got louder and louder. Filling my body with a gentleness I had never felt before. My body felt warm, like I was wrapped in a blanket of music. I felt safe and peaceful all at once. Something I hadn't felt in a long while. I let the beautiful tune lull me deeper into a trance. I swayed side to side and the tune coursed through my body. It felt like I was free falling into darkness as the weight of the world came crashing down on me.

When I opened my eyes again, it was morning.

# Chapter 35

My back ached from sleeping hunched over Luke's bed. His hand was warm in mine and he was still sleeping peacefully. I looked around the room and stretched my arms up above my head. I kissed Luke's hand and stood to walk out of the tent. I needed a fresh change of clothes and to find Daniel. I had almost made it to the door when I heard a leafy crunching coming from the corner of the tent. I turned to see the healer from last night sitting at a low table. She used a mortar to grind up some herbs. She had brilliant black and grey ringlets that fell past her backside. Half of it had been swept up into a messy bun at the back of her head. Some loose ringlets fell around her face. A face that had seen many seasons come and go. Her skin was pale and thin with age as she mixed her potion. I wondered how long she had been a healer. How many lives she had saved. And how many lives she had taken. I silently walked towards her and stopped a step away. She barely looked up from her work. Like her muscles remembered what to do before her mind did, as she added different things to the mortar and crunched them into a powder.

"What was the tune you were humming last night?" I asked, barely a whisper.

She stopped mixing and looked up at me. Her eyes were dark, though there was no wickedness in them. Her kind face gave nothing away as she looked over my own. She had deep lines across her aging skin and her lips were closed into a tight line. She began mixing again as if she hadn't heard me at all. I knelt beside her and she reached for me, startling me. Her calloused hand grasped my own and she pulled me close to her with such force that I gasped. She didn't look like a frail old lady, but she surprised me with her strength as she pulled me close.

"It is an old tune." She spoke hoarsely but softly. "It is a healing song."

"It's beautiful." I whispered.
I stared into her eyes and got lost in the galaxy that swam amongst the darkness of them. Speckles of white stars shining bright against a blacker than black sky. And as if she felt my eyes reaching into hers, she looked back down at her work.
"I have heard it before, but I can't remember where." I said.

"I am one of very few healers like me. It is a sacred song to us. Unlikely you know of it." Her voice croaked out.

I nodded. Looking over to Luke and standing to leave again.

"Please let me know when he wakes." I said to the healer and she nodded once.

I made it back to my tent and found a fresh change of clothes neatly folded on the foot of my bed and a bucket of cold water and cloth to wash. After washing and changing, I set out to find Daniel. I walked between the tents and took in the joy of the camp. Watching the people move about with such purpose. Once I made it further into the camp, I found the large gathering tent and hoped to find Daniel in there. It was still early enough that they were serving breakfast, so I found a plate and headed to the buffet table which was now lined with warm fresh bread, some jams and a bowl of fruit. I filled my plate and found a seat near the edge of the tent. I hadn't seen Daniel in here, but I figured I needed to fill my stomach first anyway.

Once I had finished my breakfast, I helped the kitchen clean up the dishes and then headed back out into the camp to try to find Daniel. I couldn't remember which tent was his, but I knew the general direction from when Jax took me. I slowly walked past each tent and peered in.

"Melody." A voice called from behind me. I turned to see Jax jogging over. "Hey! I have been looking for you all morning." He puffed out as he reached me.

"Is everything okay?" I asked quickly.

"All is fine. Tobias wants to see you." His eyes took me by surprise again, they were beautiful. One shone a brilliant light blue and the other eye a golden brown. The morning sun brightened them even more. He raised his eyebrows when I stared at him and I blinked my daze away.

"Sorry, I was with Luke. I've been looking for Daniel, have you seen him?"

"He is with Tobias and the others." He smiled. Gesturing with his hands to follow him.

I fell into step beside him and we walked through the camp, back in the direction I had come.

"How come you don't wear a pendant like some of the others?" I asked. I had noticed some of the rebels wore the same black stone pendant as Luke.

"I don't shift. So, I don't need one." He replied merrily.

"You don't shift into a creature?"

He shook his head. "Nope, I am just a plain old human." He chuckled.

"But why are you here fighting for them then?"

"My parents were creatures." His voice turned low. "They owned a mechanical repair shop in the city. Right near where the explosion happened. They were some of the first to shift."

I felt the grief that seemed to swallow up all the air. He had lost his parents to all of this. Just like Daniel and me.

"How old are you Jax?" I asked to change the subject. We passed a small fire and it hissed loudly.

"I turned sixteen a few months ago." He said, puffing out his chest proudly.

"Sixteen? My gosh, you're so young." I said under my breath.

"Hey! I'm not *that* young. Besides, I am one of the best fighters. Just ask anyone!" He raised his voice in defence.

I laughed, "I am sorry if that offended you, I didn't mean to. I just meant that, to be going through all of this." I pointed around the camp. "To be fighting with the rebels. It's a lot for anyone, let alone someone so young."

He nodded in agreement. "How old are *you*?" Jax asked, avoiding my gaze.

"I'll be turning twenty-one soon." I replied. I had almost forgotten that my birthday was coming up.

"You're still pretty young too." Then he stopped walking and reached for my arm, stopping me too.
"You have been through a lot. We all have. But together, we will be able to put a stop to it. So, *your kind* can live harmoniously with my people, as one." He smiled and continued walking.

I stood for a moment considering his words.

*Your kind.* He had said. *My* kind. The creatures are who I am now. There was no way that I would be just human again.

"C'mon. Tobias doesn't like to wait." Jax laughed and I caught up to him.

~~~

We sat around a large rectangle table for hours. Going over every single detail that happened in the lab. Tobias sat at the head of the table. His elbows rested on the tabletop with his chin on his closed fists. He only spoke when he asked me to repeat something or clarify what I had meant. I went over the past few weeks again and again. My mind felt like a jumble of words and my memories began to merge together.
~~~

"I think we should take a break for lunch." Daniel said, sensing my fatigue.

Tobias and his second and third in command nodded in unison and stood from the table. His second, Farris, was a tall and large man. Covered in muscles. He wore black fighting leathers, the same as most of the scouting team. His hair was short and dusty brown, with matching stubble across his chin and face. He was a man of few words, but his eyes were like daggers when they found you. Tobias' third in charge, Victor, wasn't tall but was built of muscle. He had a bald head, covered in tattoos. His face was feral, deep frown lines and he always wore a nasty snarl across his face. He spoke scarcely too, only when spoken to by Tobias. The rest of the scouting crew was just as intimidating. With every size, shape and colour ranging throughout the team. Most of them wore black, but some had the rebel green and brown colours. Only some wore the black stone pendants too.

When I stepped out of the tent and into the fresh air of the forest, I hadn't realised how stuffy it was in there. I had a slight headache forming in my temples and my stomach grumbled. I was a mess.

"Let's go get something to eat, then we can go visit Luke." Daniel said as he too stepped out of the tent.

"I like that plan. I am starving." I said, holding my fingers to my temples.

"Headache?" He asked. I nodded and walked alongside him. "The healers can give you something for that. A tonic."

Daniel scrambled up some chicken, fresh bread and an apple each from the gathering area and met me in front of the healers tent.

"You're doing really well Mel. Tobias just needs to know all the information so we can attack."

"*We? Attack?*" I laughed. "Look at you, switching sides so quickly."

I still didn't know the full extent of how Daniel was involved with Dr Gelch. But it rubbed me the wrong way, knowing that he aided that man with his cruel torture machines.

"I'm sorry Mel." He said and I believed him. "I am so damn sorry for everything." He took a bite from his chicken sandwich.

"Once the rebels have all the information, they can put together a plan. A plan that is going to help all creatures."

"And what are you proposing *we* do?" I retorted.

"We were going to Illumina anyway. So, why not join forces with the rebels and actually *do* something about this? You're a creature now, so is Luke. We need to fight the armies and put a stop to their plans. Make it safe for the creatures, for you."

He vanished into the healer's tent. The words hit me like a wall. We wouldn't ever be safe. Not really. Even if we went to Illumina, there would always be people trying to hunt us. Kill us. Or capture us. I followed Daniel into the healers tent and strode over to Luke's bed.

He stopped at the foot of the bed and kept his voice low as he said, "You know better than anyone the kinds of things they do to the creatures. To you. They will have more labs, Mel. The scouting teams think they may have found another one already. They're not going to stop."

I sat down next to Luke and held his hand tightly. "I'll think about it." I said without looking at Daniel.

The memories of what happened down in the lab haunted my dreams. And there might have been others, more labs and more experiments. More horrors.

Daniel stayed long enough to tell the healer I had a headache and then he slipped out. I stayed next to Luke's bed while I ate my lunch and watched the healer at work.

Again, she added different ingredients from her collection to the mortar and ground them up into a powder. Then she added some liquids and stirred them up, pouring the contents into a small teacup. I watched her as she stood from her mat and walked over to me. She limped on her right leg and I wondered what sort of injury even a healer couldn't heal.

"Hear you go. Drink it all." She handed me the cup and I thanked her.

Tipping the cup to my lips. I gulped down the small amount of liquid and coughed as the taste hit the back of my throat.

"Peppermint." She laughed and returned to her work.

The potion was strong, the peppermint filled my senses, but it was not the ingredient that had taken me off guard. I couldn't place it. There were other things at work here.

My headache had vanished within a few moments. I sat with Luke for some time. Watching his chest rise and fall and tracing the black curls of his hair. I knew Daniel was right, I just didn't know what Tobias planned to do. We had already almost died trying to escape the lab. Clear headed, I kissed Luke on his cheek and left the healers tent in search of Daniel.

# Chapter 36

Daniel had found his place in the rebel group easily. He made himself valuable with his self-taught engineering skills and knowledge of weaponry. They put him to work immediately.

He had a much nicer set up here than the small basement one he had made for himself back at home. Daniel used to scavenge, steal or trade for random objects that he thought might be useful to his work.

But the rebels had a whole tent filled with anything he could possibly need. I walked into the tent and looked over it in amazement. Both walls on either side were covered with drawers and shelves that were filled with neatly organised items. Then there was a huge work bench in the centre. Big enough to comfortably fit four workers and their creation on it.

Daniel was sitting at his station with bits of metal and tools scattered around him. Hunched over slightly and concentrating hard at the object in his hands.

My heart fluttered at a memory that tugged on my soul. From when we were only children, Daniel sat on the dining room table, creating his first invention, and working late into the night. It was a table light for our fathers study at home. He used to work late into the night and our mother always complained when he left the overhead light on. So, Daniel created a dim light to sit on the desk and attach it to our fathers laptop. It was connected by a few wires and only turned on when the laptop was in use. *Such a clever invention*, our father had told him. He was so proud of Daniel and anything he created. I walked towards him and leaned on the table.

"This brings back some memories." I said casually.

As expected, Daniel didn't reply, focused on his work. His face was tense as he twisted some wires around and around.

"You're right. I think we should do something about this." Daniel looked up from his work and raised his eyebrows at me. "You took a leap of faith coming on this journey with me, it's only fair that I return that trust. Plus, it's the right thing to do." I said.

"I knew you'd come around." Daniel nudged me. "Eventually."

I left Daniel to his work and wandered the camp again. I wasn't sure what I was going to do in the rebel group, how I was going to make myself useful.

I knew that I would figure it out eventually.

I found myself at the edge of the camp, looking out into the forest. It seemed so quiet and mysterious compared to the busy camp behind me.

Night was falling and the air was becoming icy. I felt a cold breeze brush through the forest and cool my face. The scent of fresh earth filled my nostrils and I followed it towards the tall trees surrounding the camp.

I stopped to take in the enormous trees around me and I hadn't noticed how far I'd wandered into the forest. The camp was but a whisper through the dense foliage. The rich brown earth felt soft beneath my feet.

I removed my clothes, quietly and slowly.

Not even realising what I was doing until I was running.

*Sprinting through the forest while my skin bubbled over my muscles. My bones snapped under me as I shifted while I ran and ran. The world around me became a blur of different greens. As I collapsed down onto all fours, still sprinting. My fingers contorted into long and spindly talons. My nails dug deep into the earth.*

*I roared into the sky as my body finished shifting.*

*Painless, effortless as if I had always been this way.*

*My body felt strong, sturdy as I twisted between the trees and dodged rocks that stood out of the ground. I panted hard. Smelling the different scents that filled the forest and everything surrounding it. As I slowed and looked up at the sky, I noticed some small stars had started to appear.*

*A twig snapped behind me and I jerked my head towards the sound.*

*A small, mutated rabbit hopped unsteadily across the animal path ahead of me. I followed it into the darkness. The rabbit had fungus-like mutations covering one side of its body and one of its hind legs. Making it wobble from side to side with its movements. The small animal stopped next to a little pond of water and took a drink. I smacked my lips in thirst and walked up behind the rabbit. It turned to face me and scurried off in a terrified hurry. Tripping over its mutated body.*

*I came to the side of the pond and looked in to see a dark creature staring back at me. I had never seen myself as a creature before.*

*But my ocean blue eyes were unmistakable.*

*I looked terrifying.*

*My hairless head and dark grey skin reflected to starry sky above. Long, sharp teeth jutted out of my deadly mouth. My deep blue eyes were the only tell that I was once human. I stared at my reflection, taking in the details of the creature that stared back. I lapped at the water and observed the forest around me. The noises and colours seemed so much more intense with my heightened senses.*

*After some time, I ran back to the edge of the campsite.*

*When I found my dumped clothes, I began shifting back. My skin started bubbling first, then my bones snapped and cracked as they changed shape. The shift that once used to cause pain and suffering, now felt natural. Like something I was born to do. My skin colour changed last.*

*And I watched every inch of it as it changed from a beautiful dark grey to my pale human skin.*

I pulled my clothes back on quickly as the air nipped at my bare skin and walked a few meters back into the camp. As I was tying up my leather belt again I heard a voice calling for me.

"Melody! Melody!" Jax yelled from far into the camp. I turned to jog back through the tents and saw Jax looking around.

"Jax!" I shouted back.

"It's Luke, he's awake." He puffed out.

# Chapter 37

I sprinted as fast as I could to the healer's tent and ran through the open door. I stopped dead in my tracks when I looked at Luke's bed and he was sitting upright, sipping a steaming cup. His face illuminated by a lone flame, casting a shadow across one side of it. My knees felt like they would give out if I moved, so I stood there, unmoving.

"Luke?" I spoke barely more than a whisper. He turned to face me and a smile filled his face. My heart thumped in my chest and a wave of relief washed over me as I exhaled and found the courage to take a step towards his bed. And another step and then another, before I was kneeling at his side. A sob escaped me and I grabbed his hand tight.

"Hi." He said. Squeezing my hand back.

"Hi." I smiled.

He cupped my face with his hand and I leaned into his touch, savouring it. He brought his lips to mine softly, then pulled away.

"What have I missed?" He laughed.

I filled him in on the past few days and he listened with concern. We spoke well into the night, losing track of time. He didn't speak as he let me explain everything that had happened. I only stopped once, to help him sit up further and swing his legs over the bed. I continued, and when I was finished, he sighed and took it all in.

"So, we are now part of one of the rebel groups for Illumina and we are going to fight against the armies and labs to put an end to this whole thing. Have I got that right?"

"That's the general idea, yes."

"At least it's nothing hard then." He joked and laughed.

Gods, I missed his laugh. I smiled and leaned in for another kiss. His lips pressed against mine and he held me close. Butterflies fluttered in my stomach, and I smiled under his lips.

"He needs to get up and stretch his legs soon." The healer said. And we pulled away from each other, giggling.

I wrapped my arm around his waist and Luke slung his arm around my shoulders. I helped him stand up with the weight of him on my shoulder. It was comforting to have him so close to me again. He stood unsteady for a moment before braving a step forward. His muscles were weak and sore from disuse. I helped him walk laps around the healers tent, until he was walking by himself. Only stopping to catch his breath and rub his thigh muscles. We went over the last few days a couple of times and I only had an answer for some of his questions. The night had turned into morning twilight and although the sun hadn't risen yet, we could hear the beginnings of the new day starting outside the tent.

"I think we should find Daniel and talk to him to figure the rest out." I said as Luke reached his bed and sat on the edge of it. "Maybe you should talk to Tobias too."

"I don't know about that." He said.

"I thought Tobias was one of your Hero's?" I said, confused.

"Yeah, he saved my life once. I'll always be grateful for that. I am just not sure if he would feel the same way about seeing me."

"What do you mean?" I probed.

"It's nothing." He brushed his hand through his curly black hair and leaned back on the other.

Before I could question any further, shouting came from outside the tent. I shot up and ran to the door.

"Melody, wait!" Luke yelled after me, but I was already outside and into the commotion on the other side.

People were running in every direction. It was hard to see anything in the dark morning light. Shouting and orders were heard over the chatter and yelling. It was chaos. I searched the crowd for a familiar face, anyone I could ask what was going on. Then I saw one of the women, Claire, who worked in the kitchen and raced over to her, pushing my way through and past people. I met Claire yesterday, when I helped to clean the dishes at breakfast.

I reached out and held her elbow, getting her attention. "What is going on?" I asked her.

"The scouting team has just come back." She replied, eyes wide. "We are to gather in the common tent for a debrief." She ran off back into the sea of scrambling people.

I ran back over to the healers tent and found Luke standing at the entrance, using one of the tent poles to steady his wobbly legs.

"The scouting team has come back with news." I relayed to him.

"Good news?" He asked.

"I don't think so." I said.

~~~

The entire camp was called into the gathering area and told to quiet down. Small lamps had been lit inside the tent, to allow some light inside. The sun still needed to rise over the hills in the distance. I held Luke as we followed the crowd into the tent. People spilled in and found a place to sit or stand. They opened the doors on either side of the tent so they could fit more people. I hadn't realised the sheer size of the rebel group. Hundreds of heads bobbed around, whispering and chatting as we waited. Luke and I finally made it to the congregation and stood just outside the tent. He kept his arm over my shoulder and I held his waist tightly.

To help him of course, but also because I didn't ever want to let him go again.

"Quiet down." A voice bellowed.

I stood up on my toes to try to see who spoke, but it was no use.
~~~

"Farris." Luke whispered into my ear as if he had read my mind.

Farris and Victor, Tobias' Second and Third respectively, already stood at the front of the tent. The whole mass of people silenced immediately and they looked to the front of the tent where the two men stood. Farris and Victor stared out into the crowd silently. From the corner of my eye I saw Tobias, flanked by two other men from the scouting team, walking towards the tent.

In silence, the crowd parted down the middle, allowing them to walk straight through and to the front.

When Tobias reached the front, he turned, clearing his throat and began.

# Chapter 38

Murmuring and whispers started as soon as Tobias finished explaining what they had encountered.

"Quiet!" Farris yelled over the frantic whispering.

Tobias held his hands up in the air to get everyone's attention back to him. "I know how this sounds. But we will come up with a plan, just as we always have."

"What are we going to do?" Someone yelled from the crowd and I could feel Victor's glare cut right through that poor man.

Tobias cleared his throat again and continued. "What we need now, is for everyone to continue with their daily duties and once we have a plan," he gestured to his scouting team and advisors, "we will meet back here and discuss further."

"But..." Another voice started.

"No questions. You heard Tobias!" Farris' voice was stern enough to silence anyone else. Then the scouting team and advisors stormed out. People began whispering as they too disbursed. Either going back to their duties as commanded or seeking a moment alone in their tents.

"What does this mean?" I said to Luke.

"It means that this is just the beginning." He replied, his tone was solemn.

Luke and I made our way back to the healer's tent. I helped him into his bed and we sat in silence for a few moments before he spoke.

"I knew this would happen." He spoke through gritted teeth. "I knew that they wouldn't stop."

"Tobias hardly believed me when I told him what happened in the lab." I replied quietly.

"And now he has seen it with his own eyes. The lengths they will go to. To create an army of creatures for their own use."

~~~

That afternoon, Luke, Daniel and I stood on the top of a slope that looked over the rebel camp. We had spoken very little to one another since the meeting this morning. Midday came and sun beams pierced through the clouds, shining brightly on the camp below. The cool breeze nipped at my cheeks and with every exhale, swirls of misty breath formed in front of my face. I leaned into Luke, his arm tightly wrapped around me. Daniel standing on my other side. The uncertainty of our future weighed heavily on all of us.

Luke squeezed me close and said to no one in particular, "Together. We can do this together." Then he kissed the top of my head and pulled me closer. Daniel nodded his approval
~~~

and began walking back into the camp. Ready to prepare in whatever way necessary.

I wasn't sure what tomorrow would bring, but I knew that no matter what, I would fight for these people.

For a better world.